MATTERS OF
LIFE & DEATH

MATTERS OF
LIFE & DEATH

AND OTHER STORIES

Bernard MacLaverty

JONATHAN CAPE
LONDON

Published by Jonathan Cape 2006

4 6 8 10 9 7 5 3

Copyright © Bernard MacLaverty 2006

Bernard MacLaverty has asserted his right under the Copyright, Designs
and Patents Act 1988 to be identified as the author of this work

First published in Great Britain in 2006 by
Jonathan Cape
Random House, 20 Vauxhall Bridge Road, London SW1V 2SA

Random House Australia (Pty) Limited
20 Alfred Street, Milsons Point, Sydney,
New South Wales 2061, Australia

Random House New Zealand Limited
18 Poland Road, Glenfield,
Auckland 10, New Zealand

Random House South Africa (Pty) Limited
Isle of Houghton, Corner of Boundary Road & Carse O'Gowrie,
Houghton 2198, South Africa

Random House Publishers India Private Limited
301 World Trade Tower, Hotel Intercontinental Grand Complex,
Barakhamba Lane, New Delhi 110 001, India

The Random House Group Limited Reg. No. 954009
www.randomhouse.co.uk

A CIP catalogue record for this book is available from the British Library

ISBN 9780224077859 (from January 2007)
ISBN 0224077856

Papers used by Random House are natural,
recyclable products made from wood grown in sustainable forests;
the manufacturing processes conform to the environmental
regulations of the country of origin

Typeset in Sabon by Palimpsest Book Production Limited,
Polmont, Stirlingshire

Printed and bound in Great Britain by
Mackays of Chatham plc, Chatham, Kent

*In memory of my mother
and for Maddy Skye Macdonald*

CONTENTS

CONTENTS

ON THE ROUNDABOUT

I suppose it's about doing something without thinking. But it was nothing really. Anybody'd've done the same.

We were driving back into Belfast – we could have been in Omagh or Enniskillen – visiting Anne's aunt maybe. But that's not important. It was the early seventies and that *is* important. Not long after Bloody Friday – nine dead, God knows how many maimed – all courtesy of our friends, the Provos. So everybody was a bit hyper.

It was beginning to get dark. I hadn't been all that long at the driving and I was feeling the family man – Anne in the passenger seat, the two kids in the back – like something outa Norman Rockwell. Seat-belts weren't compulsory but we were seat-belt kinda people. Clunk, click every trip – remember that? I'm thinking about what we have to do before we can relax – get the kids ready for bed – I remember all this very vividly, the way you remember just *before* a crash. Tell them a story maybe. They were the age for stories – wee Kate was anyway – at that time she made you get every word right. Any deviation and she'd have been up in arms. Sean was just talking and no more. The other thing was that the car radio was on and they were saying that the UDA were out in force in certain places – stopping and searching.

So I'm driving into that roundabout, the one at the bottom of the Grosvenor Road – the one that used to be Celtic Park – and there's this guy hitching, trying to get a lift before the cars go on the motorway. And there's a bunch of the UDA appear, about half a dozen of them, wearing khaki. And they go up to talk to the guy who's hitching. I'm about fourth or fifth in the queue onto the roundabout and I'm keeping an eye on the cars edging ahead and the UDA guys. You can never tell with them. There's one guy – he's wearing a black scarf – and he produces a claw-hammer. And he whacks the guy hitching in the face with it. And down he goes. And they start laying into him for all they're worth – boots, the hammer, the lot. There's only a couple of cars in front of us now and they scarper – away like the clappers – they don't want to know. And Anne is screaming did you see that? And her hands are up to her face. I put the boot to the floor, gunning the engine like, and before I know what I'm doing I'm driving up the pavement straight at the UDA. And they scatter. And they're laughing – I'll always remember that – laughing their heads off, especially the guy with the black scarf, the one with the hammer. I'm doing this before I know I'm doing it. But it's like we've rehearsed it. Anne pops her seat-belt, leans over and opens the back door. I get out and manhandle the poor bastard onto the floor of the back seat. He's not unconscious but he's not fully with it. He's bleeding all over the place. It's coming out of his eye and hitting the ceiling. Wee Kate is crying because she knows something's very wrong. The UDA guys are hanging back, still laughing. Maybe they think I'm the law or something. The Army maybe. Anyway I just want outa there. And I'm driving back onto the roundabout trying not to hit anything. I have a shammy for the inside of the windscreen and Anne's back kneeling on her seat, leaning over, pressing it up against the guy's face trying to stop the blood spouting all over the place. And I'm lucky because without knowing I take the exit to the Royal. He keeps going unconscious and I'm shouting to Anne keep him awake, keep him awake. And she's yelling at him what happened? What happened? And both the children are crying now, yelling their heads off. And he says he was just hitching home to Lurgan and they said are you a Fenian and before I could even fucking answer them I'm on the deck. Anne's saying hold that there, hold it. To stop the bleeding. And he's falling about but he's still talking. He can't understand. A minute ago he was trying to get home. He says the funny thing is I'm Presbyterian. I start laughing at this, looking over my shoulder. A Presbyterian? Even he thinks it's funny. Jesus. Then he falls backwards and his mouth opens and there's blood inside that looks black in the street lights. He begins jerking and passing out. Anne holds him up trying to steady him, holds the shammy to his wound – a hole between his ear and his eye the size of a ten-pence piece. He comes round again shouting I'm dead – they've killed me. The cunts have killed me. By this time

I'm driving up the wrong side of the road with my hand on the horn. Get out of my fuckin way – everybody thinks I've taken leave of my senses. Anyway we eventually get into the hospital and the staff take over.

It's only then I start to get angry. I try to give my name and address but the doctors and nurses don't want to know. There's a Brit soldier there with his gun and he doesn't want to know either. I've just witnessed an attempted murder and nobody wants to know. And Anne's carrying Sean and pulling at Kate. Come on, come on. She's looking ahead to me in the witness box facing the UDA across the court. We know your registration, we know your whole family.

The kids weren't affected. Sean doesn't remember a thing about it – he was too young – but wee Kate does. She was really scared and timid for a long time.

Anyway that's what Belfast was like at that time.

But about two months later there was a long letter in the *Belfast Telegraph*. The guy was outa hospital and he was trying to thank the Good Samaritan family who'd helped him on the roundabout that night. Wasn't that good of him? To tell the story.

THE TROJAN SOFA

It's dark – pitch black – and everything's shaking and bumping. I'm not scared – just have some what-if knots in my gut. What if they have a dog? That would be me – well and truly. Or a burglar alarm – with laser beams like they have in the movies. And when you walk through the beam, which you can't see, the alarm goes off in the nearest cop shop. But my Da would've asked all these questions when he was selling. He sells all over the place – fairs, car boot sales, a stall in the Markets – but quality stuff or as much of it as he can get. He's good – friendly – knows what he's doing.

'This is a good piece – worth quite a bit – as you well know.' And he'd laugh with the customer who had just paid up. 'If you'd more stuff like this you'd want to have an alarm in the house.'

'I don't like alarms,' or 'I've already got the best on the market.' And that'd be my Da clued in. 'You wouldn't want dog hairs all over good fabric like that.' 'I don't have a dog,' and that would be my Da clued in a bit more. He's a dab hand at getting people to tell him things.

I'm on my left-hand side – the side I sleep on at night –

because I know there'll not be much turning round in the foreseeable future. My knees bent only slightly. I've all my bits and pieces.

'You've bugger all to do except keep your wits about you and open the door. In this case two doors.'

I'm in my first year at grammar school. Got the eleven plus – no problem. Even though I hadn't reached eleven. That's good for a boy from the Markets. When my Da went up to the College the President told him I got the highest marks of anybody in Northern Ireland. Smart boy wanted. My Da sells anything and everything – bric-a-brac, furniture – you name it. I can hear his voice now talking to Uncle Eamon.

'Two flights of stairs and you're outa puff already?'

'It's the bloody smoking,' I hear Eamon say.

'Why don't you give it up? It was no problem for me.'

'Your right hand down a bit. Take it easy.'

I can hear the bumping of their feet on carpeted stairs.

'It weighs a fuckin ton,' says Uncle Eamon.

'Watch your tongue in front of the boy,' says my Da. I hear them both laughing.

He has very strong opinions, has my Da. A war is two sides, one against the other, he says. It's as simple as that. 'The wrong done to this country was so great that we can do *anything* in retaliation.' If it's done against the Brits it's OK by him. 'A broken phone is a British liability,' he says. 'So's a burnt bus. They're things that have to be replaced – by the English exchequer.'

That's why he likes to deal with the other side. I was there one time when he sold a three-piece suite to this guy – the most Orangeman-looking man I've ever seen. You could tell what he was from a mile away – the big fat jowls, the moustache, the accent. 'Your address, sir?' When he says the part of the town where he lives my Da looks at Uncle Eamon as if to say wouldn't you know?

'Yes – we can deliver free,' says my Da. So the next day I'm into the sofa with my gear and the hessian is stapled back onto the frame. It's usually an overnight. Next morning when everybody's away to work and the place is quiet I Stanley knife my way out and open the door. My Da and Uncle Eamon are sitting there in the van smiling. And in they come. The sofa's the first thing they lift because it has all the evidence in it – where I've bed and breakfasted. The modus operandi. Then they clear the place. And it's one up for old Ireland.

Before we did it for the first time my Da said to me, 'It's up to yourself. You can say yea or nay. I'd never force anybody to do something like this – never mind one of my own. But I must say it *is* for Ireland.'

'Ireland the Brave,' says Uncle Eamon from the sidelines.

What I'm in at the moment – so I've been told by my Da, the expert – is a Victorian sofa. It smells of dust, dry built-up-over-the-years dust. It's worse because we're on the move and everything's getting shaken up. Sneezing's a danger. There's a bump against something and I bang my head.

'Be careful,' says my Da to Eamon. 'The Major'll be none too pleased if his property comes damaged.'

'Niall won't be too happy either,' says Eamon.

That's me he's talking about. Niall. Niall Donnelly. Sometimes my Da calls me Skinny-ma-link. They set the sofa down and I hear a bell ringing in the distance. The door opens and a new English voice starts talking. This whole thing is like a play on the radio. You can hear everything but see nothing. And then a woman's voice joins in. There's a lotta bumping and angling so's they can get through the doorways – so much so that, when it goes upright, I have to hang on like grim death to the wooden frame. Like the ladder thing in the park you go hand over hand on.

'Here?' says my Da.

'There, with its back to the wall,' says the woman.

My Da rabbits on a bit with the Major and there's a lotta laughing while my Uncle Eamon goes for the clock. I can just see my Da, the way he throws his head back and opens his mouth wide enough to see his fillings. And Eamon smiling on his way down the stairs back to the van. He seems to take for ages. It's so bad the Major actually says, 'He's taking his time.'

'He'll be having a fly fag.' When Uncle Eamon does come back they all listen to the chimes and the Major sets it to the one he likes the best. He also chooses it to chime at quarter hours. They set the right time by their watches and there's the tickety sound of the clock being wound up. Eventually they go and I hear their voices getting weaker and the slam of the main door of the flat. I feel the vibration through the floor. There is silence now and I become conscious of my breathing – making sure my nose is clear. The man says something I can't hear to the woman. She laughs. I guess they are looking at the sofa. Then they go away.

I hear knives and forks and plates rattling in another room. A radio is switched on but it's posh music. They must be eating their tea. There's a great smell which makes me hungry. Bacon or meat of some sort. Or onions – I love fried onions.

It's very hard to know how much time has passed. My Da says I'm far better without a watch. You're more aware of time passing if you're always looking to check. Anyway I couldn't see a watch it's so dark. But it might be a kinda comfort to know how much longer I've gotta be in here. When I hear them actually talking in the other room I change my position. Move my leg a bit – change where the frame is biting into my backside – move my pillows around a bit. I'll eat my sandwiches in the middle of the night when they've gone to bed. My older brother says when I eat, it sounds like an army marching through muck. 'Keep your mouth closed.' Then I hear the clock chiming again. It does those chimes you hear on the news over a picture of Big Ben and Westminster. Then it bongs eight times.

My Da and Uncle Eamon had stopped the van out in the country to look the place over before they staple-gunned me in.

'How can you be so sure he's a Major?'

'Instinct,' says my Da. 'Maybe not a Major. But Army of some sort. All upper-crust Brits are. And they're as obvious as punks. Instead of a Mohican, a tweed cap. Leather shoes and that voice, that cut-glass voice.'

'If you were a Brit would you allow furniture in without checking it?' My Da didn't say anything. 'That's where they put fire bombs in the shops – down the sides of sofas.'

I'd gone over the hedge for a last pee – after drinking a can of Coke. I could see the house was a huge mansion with turrets and stuff, in among trees and gardens. It was about a mile away up a tarmac drive. My Da said the house had been turned into about ten flats by some developer. And he went on and on about the olden days and how could any one man have lived in such a place – to have it all to himself with servants tugging the forelock and kowtowing to him. Uncle Eamon spat out the van window.

When the Major and his woman finish their tea they switch off the radio and come into the room. Then the piano playing starts. Sort of rhythmic stuff. No point to it. Was it him or was it her playing? I was just glad there was something to listen to – to pass the time. I knew it was actual playing and not a radio, because sometimes the notes would stop and the same bit would be played again. Better. After a while the playing stopped. Someone was clapping – pretend applause. Clap, clap, clap.

'Bravo,' said the Major. 'Play me the Mozart.'

The piano started again. And went on and on and on.

With that kinda music, you know when the end is coming. It winds itself up. After that everything goes quiet.

I know they are in the room but I can't hear anything. So I start mouth breathing. It's quieter. I can sense someone sitting on the sofa, then getting off again. They're speaking very quietly – sorta murmuring. This goes on for ages and then they start exercising – sometimes on the sofa, sometimes on the floor. In school they have this crazy bastard of a gym teacher who has a yelpy voice. 'Running on the spot. Go!' 'Ten press-ups. Go!' And he reserves the highest and loudest note for yelping the word 'go'. Before the Major and his woman eventually stop the exercising and the gasping the penny drops. They're doing sex. Having a ride. Not two inches away. And I can't see a thing. And then they go back to the murmuring. I can't make out a single word. The clock chimes nine and the TV is switched on. The music is for the News. Somebody sits down on the sofa. The news is the usual boring stuff. When it comes to the Northern Ireland bit there are two murders. A prison officer who worked at the Maze tried to start his car and it blew up and he got killed. Boo-hoo. Lend me a hanky. The other was a drive-by shooting on the Antrim Road. A boy of seventeen had been shot and died on the way to hospital. If it's the Antrim Road he'll be one of ours. There was three explosions but nobody got hurt because there was warnings.

I'm feeling a bit sleepy but keep myself awake by sticking my fingernail into the back of my other hand. I don't think

I snore. But you can't be sure. A comedy programme comes on because there's a lotta laughing from the audience. Canned stuff. It goes on for ages. When the clock chimes eleven the Major and his wife go to bed. I hear the click of the light switch going off and I'm aware that the darkness has increased. I hear them doing things in the distance – running taps, brushing teeth, kettles clicking off when they boil. A hot-water bottle for her, maybe. After a while everything goes silent. At last I can turn. And fix my pillows. I don't even risk a wee groan. This must have been what it was like 'durin the war'. All the old ones at the stalls talk about 'durin the war'. They never stop. I reach out for my sandwiches – touch and rip the cling wrap. Ham and cheese. I normally like egg and onion but my Da said it's too risky – it would stink to high heaven. Give me away. Rosaleen made them. She lives with my Da now. I like her – she's a good laugh. My mother died of cancer when I was eight – right after my First Communion.

Chewing in the quiet like this is weird. The inside of your head is filled with noises, crunchings and squelchings – moving muscles and teeth-clicks and a roaring in your ears. And I think of myself as a mouse – the way other people hear a mouse. They sit up in bed at night and hear small noises, scratchings, pitter-patterings. 'There's the mouse,' they say. 'I must set the trap tomorrow.'

This is the third Trojan sofa I've done. The first was the worst. I was nervous and needed to pee a lot. Nearly filled the poly bag I had. Fresh piss is really warm. And – see –

trying to get the knot outa the neck of the bag when it was half full when you wanted to go for a second and third time – that was awful. Anyway it all went fine. A cinch. It was funny being in a house with Union Jacks and pictures of the Queen on the walls. Really spooky.

On Saturday afternoons I help Rosaleen with her stall and she gives me a tenner. All the books are priced in pencil on the inside leaf so it's dead easy. I seen the Major that day. My Da's stall is about three over from Rosaleen's. There was no indication as to what or who he was. Nothing remarkable about him at all – heavy-set in a tweed jacket, open-neck shirt, wavy hair getting a bit grey – but my Da knew the voice. The voice is a dead give-away. He was interested in this old-fashioned clock for his mantelpiece, paid a lotta attention to it, listened to the different chimes it could do and all. Then he took the Victorian sofa as well. And now here I am lying in the back of it ateing sandwiches. I don't wanna wash them down. As little liquid as possible. So I just knock them around inside my mouth till they go away. It takes bloody ages. I don't bother with the crusts.

At this very minute my Da and Rosaleen'll be coming back after a night in the pub. He takes pints of lager, she has her vodkas and Coke. When they come home me and my brother hang around being nice. They usually bring a crowd back with them – maybe a couple of fiddlers who can play jigs and reels, or singers with guitars. It's a bit of a laugh and when he's in good form my Da's liable to put his hand in his pocket – but he never remembers the next day. So you can try and tap him again. Rosaleen hugs us and says things like 'Yis are not mine – but I love ya.' Then she'll punch my Da if he's beside her. 'My womb cries out,' she says and everybody'll laugh.

I start to feel really sleepy now. I think about having a piss but whatever way I was up-ended coming through the door I can't find the poly bag. It's probably down by my feet somewhere. And I can't bend. I must have dozed off because I waken up halfway through the Westminster chimes. I lie there counting all twelve of the strokes that follow the tune. Then I hear a creak of a door in the distance. Somebody on the stairs.

Jesus, maybe he's rumbled me. But how? What have I just done? Did I snore? Did I give myself away somehow? Did he hear me chewing? No chance. Wait. The light clicks on and I can see faintly around me after the blackness. It must be the Major because he clears his throat. A deep sound, not a woman. He doesn't come near the sofa. So it's a false alarm. He shuffles over to where I think the mantelpiece must be. He is doing something footery because he's cursing and mumbling to himself. Then he says 'Ha!' and goes out of the room. The light goes off and I hear nothing more. What was that all about? Maybe he was sleepwalking. Did people really do that? Walk about the place sound asleep? Uncle Eamon says he woke up one night and he was standing pissing into a suitcase. Maybe the Major's turned off the chimes. And I'll be able to get a bit of shut-eye. 'Thanks and praises be to God.' Rosaleen says that all the time.

I don't remember anything much of what my mother said. She smiled a lot – or did I get that from photographs of her? Sitting in the park. On beaches. With other girls on the wee wall outside Granda's. And the styles. Her hair and her clothes – they were just embarrassing. When she died she went yellow. I seen her in the coffin. It had the lid off before the funeral. That was a thing she said, 'Yella as a duck's foot.' I can remember that. 'So-and-so had the jaundice – he was as yella as a duck's foot.' I lie thinking about her for a while. My Da seemed to take a long time to get over it. If any grown-up on the street mentioned her to me – 'Aw, I knew your mother' – I just wanted to cry. And that went on for years. I don't have very many friends. Most of them are grown up – like Uncle Eamon and the ones who come back to the house after the pub. I don't really like the friends who are my own age. Danny Breen and Eugene Magee. I fight with them a lot. They're so stupid playing. They squabble and fall out about the rules for everything. And they cheat all the time. It's impossible to knock around with them. 'You do this.' 'No I don't.' 'Yes you do – for I seen ya.' 'Ya fucking did not.' Like politicians in Stormont.

I can't sleep because I'm still fairly uptight. But I'm relaxed enough to be able to think about the way things are. The second time we pulled the scam it was a woman who owned the flat. She was high up in the Civil Service at Stormont. My Da said it was a cover for something to do with the H blocks. But when I got out of the sofa I couldn't believe the place. It was the worst I ever seen. Everything everywhere.

Newspapers and high-heeled shoes and magazines and half-drunk cupsa tea. Dirty knickers, dressing gowns, dresses and blouses flung all over the place. And tissues. I've never seen as many bunched-up tissues in my life. A fire hazard. And the only neat thing in the whole place was her manicure set and the ten wee nail clippings on a black coffee table – each one a wee arc. How will this woman know we've burgled her? She'll not know for a week. Unless she wants to watch the telly. Or play something on the video.

The smell of the dust inside the sofa for some reason makes me feel sad. It's not a bad smell. It's just sad. And it won't go away. The smell dries inside my mouth. I try to get in the habit of mouth breathing because it's quieter. And I begin to dream. I see myself dreaming in the darkness and then I wake up in the darkness. Not knowing where I am. And back to dreaming again. In one dream I'm in school and nobody in the class knows what 'onomatopoeia' is except me. But I can't put my hand up. I'm paralysed. Another dream is of me snoring. And jerking awake to stop me snoring. Rosaleen puts me in the bottom of a wardrobe and covers me with coats to keep the sound to a minimum. Then I wake up. Wide awake. I can sense it's light – morning light, not electric. I can make out areas and shades. I check where my Stanley knife is. It's one of those with a safety slide thing at the side for retracting and bringing out the blade. I should have been awake earlier. And I know there's something wrong. The first thing I hear is a man's footsteps walking away from the sofa. Quickly. I just know by the way he's walking that he's on to me. I hear him lifting the phone. He uses just one word. Police. Then he starts talking about an intruder in his house – trying to keep his voice down. I have to be quick. I get the Stanley knife and slide out the blade – stick it through the material above my head – out into the room. Then I pull hard. A kinda ripping sound. A thin line of light. A tent flap. And me getting out of it. Moving my stiff legs. Backing out. My feet are on the floor and I straighten up. My back feels like it's broke in two. I look down the hallway where the Major is on the phone. The door of the room is open and his eyes are watching me.

'Freeze.'

It's a scream that scares the shit outa me. The Major moves his arms upwards and now I can see he has a shotgun aimed at my head. The phone falls and swings on its wiggly cord. He starts to walk towards me. I see more and more clearly both barrels – two black holes – as they point straight at my face. He's as white as a sheet.

'Freeze you bastard.' My stomach swoops. Again and again. His voice is like the gym teacher's. Yelped. Because he's scared shitless. I could have been anything. So I do as I'm told. Try not to frighten him into doing something foolish. But I start to shake. I hope he doesn't notice me shaking. 'You fucking piece of shit. I've a good mind to kill you right now. Before the police arrive.' I'm still behind the sofa, between it and the wall. He walks past me and goes to the front door to check that it is firmly closed.

My heart's beating like mad. Then the clock chimes – the whole Westminster followed by nine dings. He must have turned it back on earlier. When I was asleep. Now I can hear the clock ticking. Or is it my imagination. Myself breathing.

'Do everything nice and slow or I might just pull this trigger. Put that blade down.'

Very deliberately, with my thumb, I retract the blade into the handle and set it on the seat of the sofa. It's weird. I'm gonna be shot in the face and yet the thing that annoys me most is – the room isn't the way I thought it was. It's much, much bigger. The mantelpiece is on the wrong wall and the piano – a grand piano with a big fin sticking up in the air – is over by the bay window. I didn't even know the room had a bay window. Everything's in the wrong place.

'You're a bit young for this game.' The cut-glass voice. Like Prince Charles. 'Who put you up to this?' My hands are resting on the back of the sofa. It's velvety material – gives under my fingers when I press. I haven't a clue what to do. I've never been caught before. The only advice I ever heard was my Da's. 'Whatever you say, say nothing.' But he was talking about guys getting interrogated in Castlereagh. Guys getting tortured.

Another thing – I badly need a piss. Even more since he scared me. You can see the Major is delighted when he sees what age I am. He keeps moving about. Swaggering almost – like the cat that got the cream. He begins getting some colour back in his face. His wife must be away to work because there's no sign of her. He begins talking ninety to the dozen. Still with the gun levelled at my head.

'I was just thinking I'll try out my new sofa – read the paper. At first I didn't believe what I was hearing. I kept thinking there's someone else in this room. Breathing.' He shakes his head in disbelief. 'It wasn't snoring – just long breaths. Who are you working for?'

I don't want to say anything. Don't want to give anything away. I look down, like I'm in pain. I'm pressing myself hard against the back of the sofa.

'I need the toilet,' I say.

'Oh – it speaks, does it?' He kinda smirks. 'Go in the police station.'

'I'm gonna wet myself.' He just stares at me. 'I'm gonna wet the carpet.'

He thinks about this and stares at me. Like a teacher when he hears an excuse he doesn't believe. Like he thinks there's more to it.

'Please,' I say. 'I've gotta go now.' I grip the front of my jeans to stop myself and close my eyes – tight. As if every muscle was connected – even my eyes were contributing to holding it in. The Major now sees it as a real threat. To his fawn carpet. He'd never get rid of the smell. He waves me out from behind the sofa with the shotgun. He goes in front of me and beckons me. He leads me into a panelled hallway. There are various brown doors off it. One is open and I can see office chairs in front of big drawing boards. Still my fist is bunched at my flies. The Major indicates another door. I open it but it only leads to another. In between there is a washing machine and a drier and a big wash basket.

He holds the door open with the toe of his brown leather shoe. I open the next door into the bathroom. He follows me in and nods to the toilet. I'm still burstin but I don't like taking my thing out in front of him. He sits down on the side of the bath and keeps pointing the gun at me. So I half turn my back on him and take my thing out.

But being watched this closely nothing happens. I've gone into some kinda block. I look at the wall in front of me. There's a framed diploma. What a place to hang a diploma. It's for Architecture. For somebody called Dunstan Luttrell. At the same time I'm trying to think of a plan. To get away. There's a narrow frosted glass window to my left but it looks well and truly closed. Anyway we're two floors up which is a long way down. Then when the piss starts it nearly drills a hole in the delph. It goes on and on and on – like it's never going to stop, making an awful lotta noise in the bowl.

'You sound like a man on stilts after a night on the beer,' says the Major. He's making jokes. There's no way this guy is going to shoot me if I make a run for it. And he wouldn't be fit enough to catch me. Fat bastard. Eventually I stop peeing and give myself a wee shake and put it away. I give a wee shivery shudder because of losing my central heating. I continue to stand at the toilet bowl. 'So you've been in there all night.' I nod my head before I can stop myself. Give him no information whatsoever. Maybe he's remembering doing the sex. Maybe he's embarrassed about it. If I leg it this minute, I'll have time to get down onto the road and into the van before the cops arrive. Maybe the traffic is bad. He waves the gun towards the hallway. I start to move past the mirror and the wash-basin. My face is too pale. 'Wash your hands.' I don't know whether he's kidding or not. The gun's pointing at me. I turn on the tap and wash my hands. It's that soap with the wee label that never goes away. Imperial Leather. The last thing to go is the wee label. How do they make it do that? I reach out to get the towel and he screams again.

'Do not fucking touch anything in this house. Scumbag.' I shake my hands a bit, wipe them on my jeans. He is so angry I'm afraid he might pull the trigger by accident. He goes out the door with the gun still trained on me and he waits in the laundry bit and waves me through. I decide this is the time. If I'm gonna go – I have to do it now. He won't have the balls. I open the door into the hallway and pull it as hard as I can after me. It slams. I hear him shouting. And I run. His hands are full with the gun. As I race past the sofa I lift the Stanley knife and pocket it. I get to the front door of the flat. By this time the Major is out of the laundry room and putting the shotgun up to his shoulder. Which means he's standing still and I'm running.

'Stop or I'll shoot,' he screams. The front door takes two hands. My back quakes expecting to be shot. The lower handle and the Yale lock. I get both open – all the time waiting for my head to explode. But he can't do it – he doesn't have the guts. And I'm through the door and running down the central stairs about four at a time. Steadying myself with my hand on the banisters. And out the main door and leggin it across the lawn to get cover from some trees and bushes. The speed I'm going. It's a bright day full of sunshine with a blue sky. I'm high on adrenalin. And after a night with a mouth full of dust it feels great. I want to yell 'Fuck you, Major. Fuck the Brits.' I zigzag through the wood as far as the road, looking at where my feet land, avoiding tree roots, kicking dead leaves. The sunlight flickers as I'm dancing down dips and sprinting up slopes. I spot the white of the van in a lay-by about half a mile away. I hear a police nee-naw in the distance. By the time I get to the lay-by I'm completely knackered. My Da is in the driver's seat facing the house and Uncle Eamon's having a look through the binoculars at what he thinks is a sparrowhawk hovering over the motorway. The police Land Rover trundles past heading for the big house. I'm coming up behind the van and they don't see me. I bang the side.

Uncle Eamon opens the door and looks down at me.

'Where did you come from?'

'Niall,' shouts my Da.

I jump up into the van. I can hardly talk for panting. 'Get outa here.' My Da switches on, indicates and we start driving.

'He caught me.' And I tell them the whole disaster.

*

The next morning was Saturday and we were all standing about in the Market.

'What have they got on us?' Eamon says. 'What can they prove? Was anything taken? It wasn't "breaking and entering". For there was no "breaking". And no "entering". If anything the boy was "exiting".'

'And very fast by the sound of it,' said Rosaleen.

'I'm sure the Major's in Intelligence,' my Da says.

The next thing is the cops turn up. Out of an armoured Land Rover. Machine guns, flak jackets, the whole gear. They questioned my Da and he spun them some yarn about catching me drunk on cider and beating me and falling out with me and me running away to hide in the sofa he was repairing and falling asleep and then him stapling it up and delivering it with me inside. And them all laughing the way he told it – even the RUC men. Then the cops talked to me – Rosaleen had her arm round me the whole time – and I backed up what my Da said. 'Leave the poor wee guy alone,' Rosaleen kept saying. I also told them I was very anxious to get outa the Major's house. With that man threatening me with a shotgun. And me only eleven. The cops threatened to bring me in front of a magistrate but nothing ever came of it.

About the Markets the talk was of me being the only burglar to leave his victim richer by a bowlful of piss and a couple of crusts. The Major *did* turn out to be the famous English architect, Dunstan Luttrell, like on the diploma. Not long after that his photo was all over the papers for designing an oratory for some nuns. The Press made a big thing about it. English architect, Irish nuns. Protestant–Catholic co-operation. Still my Da said the architecture was a cover story – everybody in Intelligence work had one. They like to keep us in the dark, he said.

MATTERS OF LIFE & DEATH 1

Learning to Dance

The boy sat on one of the divan beds for almost an hour without moving. At his feet the shopping bag with their pyjamas and things in it. His younger brother lay on a rug between the beds turned away from him. Nothing was said. Sounds drifted up from downstairs – the wireless was on, a mixture of distant music and talk. Doors opened and closed. Traffic hummed from the main road. At one point there was ringing.

'Telephone,' said the boy. His brother nodded. High heels clicked across the hallway and the ringing stopped and the doctor's wife spoke. Sometimes his younger brother made a noise like a pig – snuffing back and swallowing. It was revolting and he wanted to kill him. Then the boy heard someone coming up the stairs. The doctor's wife came to the half-open door and tapped it lightly with her fingernail.

'Can I come in?' The boy sat upright on the bed – his brother rolled around and looked over his shoulder. The doctor's wife stepped into the room. She leaned forward and put her hands on her knees so that her head was on a level with the boy's sitting on the bed. 'So – Ben and Tony – have you settled in?' The boys nodded.

'Do you want to go outside?' The boy on the bed thought it seemed somehow wrong.

'No,' he said. 'Thank you.'

'Into the garden for a bit. Get a bit of fresh air before lunch.' The boy had already made his decision and he felt it would be rude to change it.

'I'm OK.'

'Whatever suits. Also I was wondering if you had any likes or dislikes for lunch? Either of you. It's coming up to that time.' No. Both boys shook their heads. 'Some boys can be very picky. I have nephews who would run a mile rather than eat a soft-boiled egg.'

'Some eggs have elastic bands in them,' said the boy on the floor.

'Pardon me?'

'In the white bit – some brown rubbery things. Eucch.'

'Well the eggs we get here don't have anything like that in them.' She laughed. 'So what would you like?' The boy on the bed raised his shoulders in a slow shrug – he'd no idea. 'A boiled egg? With plenty of hot buttered toast?' said the doctor's wife. The boys nodded. When they had a boiled egg at home their mother spooned it from the shell into a cup and mashed the bits up with some butter so that the yellow and the white mixed evenly.

'Very well, then – it's too early, but let's go.' She ushered them out of the room and down the stairs into the kitchen. They walked quietly in their new surroundings. She sat them up on stools at a table and bustled around putting on a saucepan of eggs, dropping slices of bread into the shining toaster, setting salt and pepper on the table. There was a refrigerator as tall as herself in the corner. Every so often its engine shuddered to a halt and there was silence. She promised they would make flavoured lollipops later on.

'What's your favourite flavour?'

'Orange,' said the boy.

His brother said, 'Milk.' The doctor's wife laughed, said it was impossible to make a milk lollipop.

She was dressed as if she was going out for the evening – a silky green frock, pearls around her bare neck, high-heeled sandal shoes. She lit a cigarette from the lighter she used to light the gas and bit down hard on the first intake of smoke.

'Dr D'Arcy and his wife – they're always immaculate,' their mother had said. 'For all the world like Fred Astaire and Ginger Rogers.' Dr D'Arcy wasn't their doctor – just a friend of the family. Ben and Tony's father and Dr D'Arcy were both in the Young Philanthropists. Their own doctor was Dr Gorman. Dr Gorman was the one who came to the house when anyone was sick. And to the hospital after you had had your tonsils out.

'Ice cream – and plenty of it,' was the medicine he prescribed.

The boy had seen photos of Fred Astaire and Ginger Rogers dancing in the movies. His mother and father were very keen on supper dances and would go to one or two every year – mostly ones run by the Young Philanthropists.

For days beforehand the house would be full of excitement. On the night, the boys would be sitting in the kitchen with Grandma and Granda. Upstairs the bathroom would be going full tilt, the steam and the shaving and the powdering and perfuming all going on at the same time along with shouts of 'Are there no laces for these shoes?' 'Where are the cuff-links?' 'They'll be where you left them last year.' Dr D'Arcy would be picking them up by car, or a taxi would have been ordered and the ones getting ready would always be running late. And then they'd arrive into the room for the 'showing off' with his mother saying 'I'm as ready as ever I'm going to be.' And she'd swish and twirl around the kitchen, the dress and her petticoats taking up most of the small space. She'd touch the necklace at her throat and worry that it didn't match her diamanté bag. His father would straighten his black bow-tie at the mirror by crouching his knees. It was set at the correct height for their mother. And because it was a special occasion they'd kiss the boys goodbye and tell them to behave and so on and not give Grandma any trouble. Their father smelt of shaving soap. And their mother would decide at the last minute not to wear a coat because it just made the dress underneath look silly – her wrap would be warm enough. And the doctor's car would be honking its horn outside and suddenly the door would rattle and slam and they'd be gone. Silence. And Grandma and Granda would be sitting opposite each other smiling, waiting to play cards. The next morning when the boys woke there would be balloons and paper hats and brightly coloured cocktail sticks shaped like tiny sabres on their bedside chairs.

'You poor things,' said the doctor's wife. Her long red hair gave the impression of being unruly – standing out as it did from her head. She fought a constant battle with it combing and sweeping it aside with open fingers.

'Four minutes?' she said. 'To be on the safe side?' She looked very tall and glamorous as she stood waiting for the toast with one hand on her hip and a cigarette in the other. Her fingernails were painted. Even her toenails were scarlet – peeping out the front of her high-heeled sandals. When the eggs were ready she set one in front of each boy. They stared at them but didn't move.

'Let me.' She sliced the top off each egg and set it on a plate beside the eggcup. 'No bits of shell,' she said. 'Clean as a whistle. And apostle spoons. What's keeping you?' The boy scooped a little egg white from the lid and put it in his mouth. His younger brother did the same. The doctor's wife took a seat on a stool and leaned her elbows on the table staring at her guests. She looked long and hard at them then smiled.

'I would just love two boys like you,' she said. There was a sound of crunching toast and chewing. She made a platform for her chin with her fists and looked from one boy to the other. The younger boy chewed his food with his mouth open. His brother watched in disgust as he rolled the mashed-up food around his mouth. Occasionally the younger boy stopped for breath – breathed in past the mush and then would continue chewing.

'So what would you like to do this afternoon?' The boys continued to eat and stare defiance at each other. 'We could do something in the garden.'

'Like what?' said the boy. He must have thought his reply sounded rude because he added, 'That'd be OK.'

'What games do you play at home?' The boys stared down at their eggs then looked at each other. The boy said with a smile, 'Cricket in the yard.'

'I'm afraid we have no yard here.'

'Slow-motion football,' said his brother.

'And what, may I ask, is that?'

The elder boy tried to explain – a round balloon – the pitch was the hall – the goalposts were the front door and the width of the stairs. His younger brother got off his stool and began to move in the kitchen with heavy limbs demonstrating to the doctor's wife. He was smiling, remembering. 'Like you're in syrup when you head the balloon – it's slow motion – like in the pictures.'

'I'm sorry but we have no real toys – not even a balloon.' The kitchen darkened and spots of rain appeared on the window pane.

'We'll have to think of something else. Would you look at that?' She nodded outside. 'How I would love to live somewhere like Spain or Barbados. Somewhere you can depend on the weather.' The boy's brother took a spoonful of egg and looked down into the shell. He made a noise in his throat – he didn't spit – but he allowed the egg along with some half-chewed toast to tumble out of his mouth onto his plate. He drooled strings of liquid stuff after it. His brother turned away.

'Is anything wrong?' said the doctor's wife.

The younger boy was leaning forward, swallowing and swallowing. 'An elastic band,' he said looking down into his eggshell.

'No. There's no such thing.' The doctor's wife swivelled off her stool and came to see. The child pointed at a small brownish spot deep in the white of the egg and curled his lip.

'Would you like a banana?' She took the plate with the mouthful of mush and tipped it into the bin as if nothing had happened.

'Thank you,' he said when she set a banana on his plate. He peeled the skin back and scrutinised the white of the banana for flaws or ripe spots.

'I hope the rain's not on for the day,' said the doctor's wife. 'More tea?' Both boys refused. 'When you're finished in here – you can just wander about the place. Explore the house.' The telephone rang in the hall and she hurried out. They heard her talking for a long time. When she came back they had finished eating.

'You can go anywhere you like, boys, except the surgery. Dr D'Arcy sees his private patients in there. Need I say more? Needles and things.' She gave a little shudder. 'It's the only room we keep locked. Let me show you around.' She ushered them out of the kitchen and led them along a parquet hallway. She left wafts of lavender in her wake.

'Oh, this is what we call the dancehall.' She pushed the open door and the boys looked in. It was a yellow wooden floor. There was a large bay window which made the room seem very bright. They all walked into the room and suddenly there was an echo to every sound.

'This is a maple sprung floor – our one extravagance. It was put in by the same people who did the Plaza Ballroom. Feel it move with you.' She let her hand rest on what looked like a sideboard. 'The radiogram. The piano is for visitors who can play. Can either of you?'

They both shook their heads. No, they couldn't. They went to the next room.

'This is the library but not many children's books, I'm afraid.' She pointed to one side: 'Mostly medical stuff. Not very nice. Promise me you'll avoid that side.' The boys agreed. 'But the good Doctor likes the occasional detective story.' She waved her hand at a bookcase full of green-banded paperbacks. 'Most of all, Agatha Crispy.'

'Christie,' said the elder boy.

'Just my little joke.' She smiled and pointed out some of her own childhood books, but they looked schoolgirlie. The telephone rang and she rushed to answer it shouting over her shoulder, 'I'll leave you to it.'

The boy and his brother stood staring at the detective stories. The older boy turned to the forbidden medical books at the other side of the room. They had titles he could barely read. Words that meant nothing to him – ologies and isms. There were *Lancet*s and *British Medical Journal*s, many books about 'the Catholic Doctor', shelves full of Maynooth and Down and Conor quarterlies, the yellow spines of countless copies of *National Geographic*. He took down a large book and opened it. It had some black-and-white pictures illustrating diseases. Misshapen men stripped to the waist. A person with a blackened hairy tongue thrust out. A bare woman with droopy chests covered in spots. Then babies stuck together – then things so horrible he slammed the book shut and put it back on the shelf.

He went into the dancehall, hoping to get away from such images. But they were in his head. He knelt down on the smooth floor to look at what records there were. They were neatly stored in heavy books which contained paper sleeves with a circular window so that the label could be read. Decca, Columbia, Parlophone and His Master's Voice – the rich red behind the white dog. The radiogram had a cupboard at one end and the door was not properly closed. The boy looked around then eased it open. Bottles and glasses. A bar stocked with gin and whisky and other stuff.

He turned round and his brother was standing there with his hands in his pockets. He pushed the cupboard door shut.

'What are you standing there for?' His brother pulled a face. 'Why don't you go somewhere else?'

'I'm all right here.'

'Why d'you always have to follow me?'

His brother didn't move for a while. Eventually he sidled off back into the hallway. It was good to be rid of him. His very presence was an annoyance – the way he spat out his food in front of the doctor's wife was terrible. But it wasn't just that – it was a continual thing. His sniffing. His mouth noises. He did sneaky farts. Sometimes you heard them, sometimes you didn't.

He went back to the library to look through the *National Geographics*. The rain had stopped ticking at the window and the sun came out. He sat down on the floor with a magazine. The light fell in warm squares on the flowered carpet. The wallpaper was strange and rich. He had never seen anything like it. It had a pattern of flowers – maroon against a creamy background. But the flowers were made of velvet. He reached out and touched the pattern with his fingers. It was soothing the way it gave when he pressed it. The words on the page seemed to move. He found them difficult to read. His eyes wanted to close. He was tired. He hadn't had much sleep. What with people running up and down the stairs all night. Sometimes loud voices, sometimes whispering outside his door. At one point he'd recognised the priest's voice. When he'd put his head out to see what was going on, his mother had pleaded with him to stay in bed. 'For me,' she said and her face had had a look he had never seen before. On anyone's face. So he stayed put with the eiderdown pulled over his head. His brother had slept throughout.

He put his head down on his forearm and closed his eyes. And he drifted in the warmth of the sun. When he awoke he smiled – then remembered and his face went solid again. He didn't know how long he'd slept for, but he had drooled on his arm. He rubbed it dry and looked around him. What must have wakened him was the slam of a car door because the back door of the house opened and a voice shouted, 'Hello!'

Dr D'Arcy, still wearing his hat, stopped at the threshold of the library and saw the boy lying on the floor.

'Hi,' he said. 'What a sad, sad day.' He came and hunkered down in front of the boy. The doctor reached out and touched him on the shoulder. Then patted him on the head as he straightened up. The boy did not know what to say. He was on the verge of tears but did not want to show it. 'You're making yourself comfortable, I see.'

'Yes.'

The doctor stepped back out into the hallway. His wife came to him and offered herself for a kiss. He took off his hat and kissed her. The boy looked away.

'Not lonely today, eh?' said the doctor.

'I have my hands full.'

'Where's the other boy?'

'In the garden.'

The doctor hung his hat on the hall stand. He was tall and thin and wore a dark pinstripe suit with a pink shirt and a maroon bow-tie. His thinning hair was Brylcreemed flat to his head. In high heels she was almost as tall as her husband.

'The weather's wonderful now.' The doctor's wife beckoned the boy. 'Let me show you the garden.'

All three of them went out the back door. The garden

was surrounded by a grey stone wall, but the boy could see other gardens with hedges and apple trees.

'It keeps the heat in and the wind out,' said the doctor's wife. 'Do you like flowers?' The boy said he did. 'Dahlias and chrysanths are my favourites. I put so much work into my flowers.'

The doctor produced a packet of Craven A and he and his wife lit cigarettes.

'I suppose you're a bit young to start,' he said and they all laughed.

As they walked around the garden she pointed out various plants and told him things about them. 'Eternal vigilance when it comes to snails,' she said. 'Japonica here. And night-scented stock. Ummm . . .' She cupped a russet chrysanthemum and inhaled its scent while making swooning noises. The boy looked at her. The parting in her hair was straight. The skin of her scalp was blue-white shining beneath her auburn hair. The doctor walked with his hands joined behind his back.

Down behind a garden shed they came across the boy's brother.

'Is that where you are?' said the doctor's wife. The younger boy stood up and looked sheepish.

'It was nice and warm here,' he said.

'What age difference is there between you?' asked the doctor's wife.

'I'm ten and a half and he's twelve and a half.'

'I know what we can do,' said the doctor.

'What?'

'A little archery.'

'No.' His wife seemed taken aback.

'The boys can use your bow. They could draw that. Easily.' The doctor walked away towards the garage and came back with a bow and a quiver of six arrows which he gave to his wife. Then he went back and came out with a target which had cobwebs hanging from it. He walked past them and set it three-quarters of the way down the garden.

'Adult toys,' he said. Then he straightened his face. 'This is not a toy. People could get killed.' He dropped his cigarette and trod it with his toe into the grass. His wife took one more inhale and did the same.

'Ask King Harold,' she said.

'He got it in the eye,' said the boy.

His younger brother clapped his hand to his eye and staggered about gasping, 'Agghhh.'

'OK – enough. Enough. Who wants to go first?'

The boy shrugged and indicated his younger brother. The doctor's wife sat down on a concrete step and crossed her legs. The doctor talked them through the equipment in such detail.

'Watch carefully. Everything I say to your brother also applies to you. This groove at the bottom of the arrow is called the nock.'

The boys just wanted to be firing arrows. Eventually the doctor took one from the quiver and notched it onto the string. He pulled the bow and aimed at the target.

37

'Make sure the string touches your lips.' He released the arrow and it flew silently and stuck in the edge of the target. 'I'm not used to your bow, darling.'

'Nothing to do with the fact that we haven't shot for about five years.'

He laughed. Then fitted the younger boy up to shoot.

'At least move the target a little closer,' said the doctor's wife. Whenever the younger boy did shoot the arrow, it slanted into the grass well to the left of the target. His brother laughed and sneered.

The doctor noticed this and said, 'I hope you can do as well.' The doctor handed him the bow, then an arrow. The arrow had a brass tip which looked like a bullet. He notched it on the bowstring and drew the bow just as he'd been shown. There was a great feeling of power – like a spring wound as tightly as it would go. He shot the arrow and it ended up in a flower-bed at the foot of the wall.

'Not bad at all. Better distance,' said the doctor.

They continued practising for some time and they all cheered loudly when the older boy's arrow stuck into the straw at the outer edge of the target. The telephone rang in the house.

'Just a minute,' said the doctor and hurried away. It was the older boy's turn to shoot. The doctor called out to his wife and as she jumped to her feet the boy saw the white undersides of her thighs. She ran inside leaving the boys alone in the garden. The boy drew the bow and aimed at the target. He held fire. The thought in his head was that it was possible to kill his brother here – in this walled garden, away from everyday life. Then there would be two funerals. He could say it was an accident. At the pictures he had seen arrows thwack into the bodies of US Cavalrymen. He could see it now – this one in his fingers piercing his brother's pale blue shirt. The blood welling and gathering around the shaft as it protruded from his chest. He slowly turned the weapon on his brother. He stood there with his mouth half open, mouth breathing, squinting his eyes against the sun.

'You're not allowed to do that,' said the younger boy.

'Where's your brother?' asked the doctor.

'In the bathroom.'

'Good.'

'So everybody's hands are washed?' said the doctor.

'Including mine,' said the doctor's wife smiling.

The younger boy came to the table with the backs of his hands glistening where he had neglected to dry them. The doctor said grace and they all bowed their heads after the doctor's wife bowed hers.

'What are you interested in?' The doctor shook out his white linen napkin and looked first at the smaller brother, then the older boy.

The silence was there until the older boy felt he had to say, 'Dunno.'

The doctor spread the napkin over his lap.

'You're at the grammar school?'

'Yes. Going on to second year.'

'Have you any hobbies?'

The boy didn't want to say he didn't know again so he said, 'Yes.'

'What?'

The boy thought for a while. Then said, 'Painting by numbers.'

'That's interesting. How many have you done?'

The boy hesitated and the younger boy said, 'One. He's done one. But he never finished it. He only did up to four.'

'I did finish it. I did all the colours.'

'He only did two of the blues and two greys.'

The doctor's wife interrupted, 'Now boys I'm sure it's not worth fighting over. What was it of?'

'A garden.'

'How I would love to have this all the time. Bickering and refereeing. You are wonderful children . . .'

'Phyllis . . .' said the doctor and she stopped talking. She looked down at her plate. The doctor lifted his spoon from the white tablecloth and began his soup. The others did likewise.

'And you, little man? What school are you at?'

The younger brother sucked in the hot soup with a slurping noise.

'I'm not a man,' he said. 'I'm in Primary Seven.' The doctor's wife smiled. As did the doctor. There was silence at the table when the two adults refused to ask any more questions. Eventually the doctor spoke.

'Your father was a great man,' he said. 'It's so seldom one person can make a difference.'

All their spoons chinked against their plates and nobody said anything for some time.

In his single bed his younger brother began crying. But he tried to disguise it – keeping it in. This started the boy off too and he cried into his pillow trying to cloak the sound he was making – a silent kind of open-mouthed girning, with tears wetting his face and the pillow. He stopped to hear if his younger brother had stopped. Silence. Except for downstairs. There was music playing. He didn't know what time it was. It was still quite light. He didn't know if he had been asleep or not.

After dinner they had played cards. Knockout Whist, Old Maid, Beggar-My-Neighbour. Then the doctor had left to drive down to the boys' house to pay his respects. The doctor's wife said it was her duty to stay at home – not to babysit, they were far too old for that – but just to keep an eye.

The boy listened hard and heard the regular breathing of sleep coming from his brother's bed. He was thirsty. He'd have to get up. Did too much crying make you thirsty? Was there a loss of moisture? He didn't want to call out as he might do at home. And he needed the toilet. He got up and went to the bathroom. Afterwards he stood at the head of the stairs and listened down. The music had stopped long ago. Lights were on all over the place but he couldn't see anyone. Where was the doctor's wife? He could be down and get his drink of water from the kitchen and nobody would notice.

He began down the runner of carpet on the black staircase. The boards creaked a little but nobody came to see who or what was making the noise. In the kitchen there were glasses in the draining rack. He filled one and sipped from it. The refrigerator made him jump by quivering into life. With the glass in his hand he moved out onto the parquet tiles of the hall. There was a ticking noise coming from somewhere – not like the ticking of a clock, it was too slow for that. He walked towards the sound. It was in the room with the dance floor. He looked in and saw the doctor's wife sitting in a tall armchair – at least he saw her legs. Her back was to the door. The lid of the radiogram was up and a record was revolving slowly – clicking in the overrun. The room was full of twilight from a yellow band in the sky. There was something about the way her legs were sprawled that looked strange. He walked towards her. Was she dead? Was it something to do with the light? He peered around the wing of the armchair. She was fast asleep, her mouth half open, her head slumped. She would wake with a sore neck if she slept like that for long. Still the record clicked regularly. He turned and with his right hand lifted the needle off. The noise stopped. Then she wakened. At first she looked glazed and bewildered, as if she didn't know where she was. Or who he was – a boy in pyjamas standing in front of her. She opened and closed her mouth drily several times.

'Oh, how thoughtful of you,' she said, taking the water from his hand. She gulped it down and sighed when she had finished. 'Thank you. Just what the doctor ordered.' As well as cigarette smoke there was a strange smell in the air. Not perfume – but like perfume. She set the empty glass down on a low table beside her chair. There were several bottles on it – a half-filled green bottle, a wine bottle – empty glasses, a half-filled ashtray. 'I'm such a mess.' She sat forward and had a double-handed scratch with her fingers through her hair.

'Where's Gabriel? Is he not home yet?' The boy didn't know so he shrugged. 'What time is it?' She squinted at her watch. 'Oh my God. A quarter to a lemon.' She turned to the small table and finished the drink in her glass and smacked her lips. She poured herself another drink and lit a cigarette. That was the perfumed smell. 'A gin is not a gin without ice,' she said and levered herself up from the armchair. She came back from the kitchen with her glass ringing and the cigarette in her mouth. 'I feel I want to dance. Will you do me the honour, Tony?' The boy didn't know what to say. 'Can you do a quickstep?'

The boy shook his head. He couldn't be rude to people who were looking after him. But he wanted to run.

'I thought not. But it's really quite easy.' She switched on a red side light and stood in front of him. 'Right. To begin at the beguinning. That's hard to say at this time of night.' She went to the table and stubbed out her cigarette. She placed her hands on his shoulders and showed him the steps.

43

Looking down she realised he was in his bare feet. 'I don't want to tread on your tootsies.' She unhooked her feet from her high-heeled sandals and kicked them to one side. Then she stood with her feet together and sighed. 'Ohh I have such bunions.'

She continued to teach him the steps and move him around. He felt ungainly and reluctant. His head was almost to the height of her shoulder and he could smell her perfume and another strange smell like onions. When he made mistakes with his feet she laughed uproariously – doubled over at times. He didn't see what was so funny. His face was hot and he was sure he was blushing. Once or twice she grazed his cheek with her breast. It was a soft feeling. It gave and he wanted to touch it again out of curiosity – like the wallpaper. 'Now music will sort the whole thing out. Listen to the music – really listen – and the dance will come to you.'

She turned away from him and played the record on the turntable. The music breathed out. '*Heaven, I'm in heaven.*' She began to sway in time to the singing voice. '*And my heart beats so that I can hardly speak; and I seem to find the happiness I seek, when we're out together dancing cheek to cheek.*' She laid her hands on his shoulders and pressured him into moving. 'No – don't look down,' she said. 'You're good – you're getting the hang of it. Move to the music.' She crooned the words along with the singer.

She said, 'Gabriel says dance is about not getting in each other's way gracefully.' Then she added as if it was an afterthought, 'I think it's about knowing – about knowing each other. And wearing gorgeous clothes. There is no sight in the world to beat a man in a dress suit. Love is everything.'

The boy tried to humour her. She made him attempt to dance again. His bare feet scuffed and bumped against the springy floor. He trod on her but she seemed not to notice. She seemed not even to be speaking to him. She said, 'For me dancing is a matter of life and death. Can you imagine what it would be like to be in an iron lung?' Somewhere a door closed but she seemed not to notice.

The doctor stood in the doorway of the dancehall room and switched on the main light which was shaped like a chandelier. She blinked and stared in his direction. He slowly removed his hat and hung it on the hall stand.

'Gabriel,' she said. 'I'm just teaching our guest the rudiments.'

'Ot-way are-hay oo-yay ooing-day?' he said.

'Othing-nay.' She took her hands off the boy's shoulders. The record came to an end and began ticking again.

'Oo-tay uch-may ink-dray.'

'No, only a little. I felt so sad when they went to bed.'

'My parents talk that language too,' said the boy.

'Of course,' said the doctor, smiling. 'I forgot – it was they who taught it to us. They said it was a code for talking in front of you.'

'But I got to know what they were saying.'

'We speak it even though we don't have any children,' said the doctor's wife.

45

'Ime-tay or-fay ed-bay. You have a difficult day tomorrow. Your mother sends her love.'

'Gabriel, dance with me. Let's demonstrate the quickstep for him.'

'Phyllis – you're being . . . The time is out of joint.' The doctor's glance went to the boy.

'Please,' she said. 'There's no time like the present.' She lurched to the side of the floor and got into her high-heeled sandals. From the window sill she took a box and sprinkled something from it whispering onto the floor.

'Lux perpetua,' she said and turned to the boy. 'Soap flakes – to allow the feet to glide.' She put the record on again. 'A bit more volume.' And raised her hand to invite the doctor to dance. He stared at her and nodded his head a little in disbelief. '*Heaven, I'm in heaven*,' and they were away across the floor, their bodies close, their feet in time. The doctor, when he turned, rolled his eyes to the boy – to let him know he was just humouring his wife who was being more than a little foolish. The fingers of their upright hands were interlaced. The doctor's hand at her back was cupped as if holding something precious. Their feet skimmed and her dress swished and outlined her thin body as she traversed the floor. The boy now knew the tune and knew where it was going. They moved as one person, their legs scissoring together to the music. They had variations – sometimes dancing side by side – sometimes swinging out away from each other and slingshotting back together again. She threw back her head and her red hair fell and swayed. The doctor's back was straight, his chin elegantly proud. The boy felt as if he was watching his parents. If they didn't dance like this – and he had never seen them dance at home because they had rugs on the floor and the room was too small – it is how they would have wanted to dance.

He felt he couldn't leave the room and go back up to bed because the doctor and his wife covered so much of the floor so quickly. He would be trampled or would at least cause them to interrupt their dancing and he didn't want to do that. So he stayed where he was and watched. He joined his hands behind his back the way he had seen the doctor do earlier in the garden and leaned back against the wall. The wallpaper in this room was also like velvet. The pattern was of green bamboo and moved beneath his hand. He caressed it behind his back as he watched the dancers.

Something moved in the doorway. It was his brother. The loud music must have wakened him. His face looked crumpled and sleepy and he stood with bare feet on the threshold.

'Dance with your brother,' shouted the doctor's wife.

'That would look stupid,' said the boy but not loudly enough for it to be heard. It was enough that at that moment he was glad he hadn't killed him in the garden earlier.

The music stopped. And the doctor and his wife ended their dance, he mock bowing and she inclining her head in gratitude for being asked. The only sound now apart from the ticking of the record was their loud breathing.

'I see we are all here now,' said the doctor looking at the boy in the doorway.

47

'I couldn't sleep.' The doctor, still panting, went over and squatted down before the boy standing on the threshold.

'I'm not surprised. At her volume,' he said and looked at his wife. 'Now boys you have a difficult day tomorrow. You'd better get some sleep.'

'I'll waken us at half eight,' said the doctor's wife.

'And I'll run all of us in for ten o'clock mass.' By now the two brothers were together at the foot of the stairs. The doctor was touching each of them on the shoulder. 'Oh, I forgot to say. Ben, Tony – it is now definite. The Bishop *will* attend the funeral. Not many people that happens to. You should be very proud. Goodnights apiece.'

The boys began the stairs. When they were halfway up the elder boy looked round. The doctor's wife was in tears, watching them climb.

THE CLINIC

It was still dark. He was *never* up at this time, except occasionally to catch a dawn flight. He picked up his sample, his
papers and the yellow card. The bottle was warm in his hand.
He was about to go out the door when he remembered.
Something to read, something to pass the time. In the room
with the book shelf he clicked on the light. The clock on the
mantelpiece told him he was running late. He grabbed a small
hardback collection of Chekhov's short stories and ran.

It was mid-November. People's Moscow-white faces told
how cold it was. Breath was visible on the air. The traffic
was ten times worse than he was used to. He turned off
into the hospital and got lost a couple of times before he
saw the Diabetic Clinic sign. He parked ages away and half
hurried, half ran back. He was breathless going through the
door only to find that the place was upstairs. He was about
eight minutes late and apologised. The receptionist shrugged
and smiled, as if to say – think nothing of it. That made
him mad too. He had been so uptight trying to get there
on time and now, it seemed, it didn't matter very much. If
there was one thing worse than worrying, it was wasted
worrying. He was asked to take a seat.

The waiting room was half full even though it was only twenty to nine. There was a row of empty seats backing onto the window. He sat down, glad not to be close enough to anyone to have to start a conversation. A Muslim woman in a black hejab talked to her mother who was similarly dressed. The language was incomprehensible to him but he was curious to know what they were talking about.

All the men's magazines were about golf or cars. He picked up *Vogue* and flicked through it. Beautiful half-naked sophisticated women clattering with jewellery. But he couldn't concentrate to read any of the text.

His letter lay face up on the chair beside him.

Your family doctor has referred you to the Diabetic Clinic to see if you are diabetic. To find this out we will need to perform a glucose tolerance test.

He remembered a crazy guy at school who had diabetes – who went into comas. But school was fifty years ago. Since being given his appointment he'd read up even more frightening stuff about your eyesight and how you could lose it. And your extremities – how in some cases they could go gangrenous and have to be lopped off.

His yellow outpatient card said *Please bring this card with you when you next attend.*

A door at the far end of the waiting room opened and screeched closed. It took about thirty or forty seconds to close, with its irritating, long, dry squeak. There was a damping device on the mechanism to make it close more slowly. But no sooner had it closed fully and the noise stopped than somebody else came through it and began the whole process over again. 'Collective responsibility is not being taken,' he wanted to yell. If he had diabetes and had to come back to this God-forsaken place then next time he'd bring an oil can. Recently in the newspaper he'd read that grumpy old men were more liable to heart attacks than old men who were not grumpy. He tried to calm down. To degrump.

He took out his Chekhov and looked at the list of contents. Something short. He did a quick sum, subtracting the page number from the following page number after each story. It was an old copy and the cheap paper had turned the colour of toast at the edges. The Vanguard Library edition – translated by the wonderful Constance Garnett. A nurse walked in and called people by their first names. She came to him.

'Hi, my name is Phil,' she said, 'and that's Myna at reception.' She explained what was going to happen. He had to drink a whole bottle of Lucozade and then, over the next couple of hours, every half hour in fact, he had to give both blood and urine samples. He nodded. He understood. He had grey hair, he was overweight, but he understood.

She took him into the corridor and sat him down in what looked like a wheelchair.

'Did you have any breakfast?' she said. 'A cuppa tea maybe? Some toast?'

'No. The leaflet said to come fasting.'

'Not everybody pays attention to that.'

'What a waste of everybody's time. Do people actually do that?'

'You'd be surprised,' she said.

It turned out not to be a wheelchair but a weighing machine. She calculated something against a chart on the wall.

'Did you bring a sample?'

'Yes.' He rummaged in his pocket and produced the bottle. It had returned to room temperature. *Spring water with a hint of Apple*. He handed it over and the nurse put a label on it.

'It might be a little flavoured,' he said.

'I'm not going to drink it.' She whisked it away into another room.

When he was back in his seat by the window she brought him Lucozade, a plastic glass and four lozenge-shaped paper tubs. She stuck a white label with a bar-code on each and wrote a time on the rim with her biro. He wanted to make terrible jokes about giving urine samples and her name. Phil. Phil these please. P for Phil. But he realised everybody must do this. He said, 'I hope these are not for blood.'

She laughed. She had a nice face – in her early forties.

'All at once now,' she said. He poured the Lucozade into the plastic glass and drank it. Refilled it, drank it. Halfway down he had to stop, his swallow refused to work against the sweet bubbles. Eventually he finished everything and childishly expected praise.

When she left him he tried to concentrate on his book. A story called 'The Beauties' looked feasible. Subtract one hundred and seventy-three from one hundred and eighty-three. It'd be hard with all this toing and froing – all the stabbing and pissing. All the people around him talking. He didn't think he'd read it before. That had happened several times with Turgenev – after fifty pages he'd said, 'I've read this before.' It went down so easily. Nobody gagged on Turgenev.

But Chekhov is Chekhov. He draws you in. He writes as if the thing is happening in front of your eyes. An unnamed boy of sixteen, maybe Chekhov himself, and his grandfather in a chaise are travelling through the summer heat and dust of the countryside to Rostov-on-the-Don. They stop to feed their horses at a rich Armenian's and the grandfather talks endlessly to the owner about farms and feedstuffs and manure. The place is described in minute detail down to the floors painted with yellow ochre and the flies . . . and more flies. Then tea is brought in by a barefoot girl of sixteen wearing a white kerchief and when she turns from the sideboard to hand the boy his cup she has the most wonderful face he has ever seen. He feels a wind blow across his soul.

'The Beauties' had captured him. He knew exactly what Chekhov was talking about. He was there in that room experiencing the same things.

At precisely a minute before a quarter to the hour he lifted one of his cardboard pee pots and went to the technician's laboratory. The technician was a woman with long brown hair who smiled at him. She wore a white coat. Her breast pocket had several biro ink lines descending into it. She explained what she was about to do.

'You can choose to have it done on four fingers. Or you can have it done on one finger four times. That's the choice. Four sore fingers or one very sore finger?'

He chose his middle finger and presented it – almost like an obscene gesture. He looked away, anticipating a scalpel or dagger. There was a winter tree outside. Without leaves a crow's nest was visible. There was a click and the stab was amazingly tiny – like the smallest rose thorn in the world. He hardly felt anything. The technician squeezed his finger and harvested his drop of blood into a capillary tube the size of a toothpick. When she'd finished she nodded at his cardboard container. He lifted it and sought out the lavatory.

The sign on the door indicated both men and women. Inside there were adjacent cubicles and the mother of the woman in the black hejab was coming out of the ladies' bearing her cardboard pot before her like an offering. He smiled and opened the outer door for her.

Inside the men's lavatory was a poster about 'impotence'. A man sitting on a park bench with his head in his hands. How did he discover his condition in a public park? *Talk to your doctor*, said the words.

Conjuring up a sample so soon after the one in the house took a long time. But eventually he succeeded and left it in the laboratory. The technician was working near the window. Her long hair was down her back almost to her waist.

'There you are,' he said.

'Thank you.'

The nurse brought him a plastic jug of tap water and ice.

'You might be able to give blood every time,' she said, 'but for the other you need to keep drinking this.'

He swirled the jug and poured himself some. It sounded hollow compared to ice against glass. Sipping he tried to return to the Chekhov. A distant radio was far enough away to be indistinct but it was still distracting. At the moment the only other sound was of magazine pages being turned – the kind of magazines which were looked at rather than read – Hello! and OK. Flick, flick, flick. The nurse, Phil, came in and announced a name.

'Andrew? Andrew Elliot?'

A man stood and swaggered forward responding as if he had just been chosen for a Hollywood audition. In a music-hall kind of American drawl he said, 'You caalled for me, lady?'

Everybody in the waiting room laughed.

He tried to return to the mood of that hot, dusty afternoon in Rostov-on-the-Don but the smile was still on his face. He couldn't concentrate.

He was at that age when things were starting to go wrong.

Knee joints were beginning to scringe. Putting on socks had become a burden. Pains where there shouldn't be pains. Breathlessness. Occasional dizziness.

An immensely fat woman came in. All her weight seemed to be below her waist. Her thighs and lower belly bulged as if she'd left her bedding in her tights. Sheets, pillows, duvets. The lot. After her, an old couple came through the doors, panting after the stairs. They sank onto chairs, incapable of speech, and sat there mouth breathing. They both had skin the colour of putty.

When he began to read again he found it awkward to turn the page because, like many people in the waiting room he had a piece of lint clenched between his chosen finger and his thumb.

The boy in 'The Beauties' when confronted with the girl in the white kerchief feels himself utterly inferior. Sunburned, dusty and only a child. But that does not stop him adoring her and having adored her his reaction is one of – sadness. Where does such perfection fit into the world? He hears the thud of her bare feet on the board floor, she disappears into a grimy outhouse which is full of the smell of mutton and angry argument. The more he watches her going about her tasks the more painful becomes his inexplicable sadness.

The first part of the story ends and Chekhov switches to another, similar incident when he has become a student. Maybe a medical student. This time he is travelling by train.

In the waiting room of the Diabetic Clinic the talk was of medical stuff.

'I have an irregular heartbeat . . .'

'Oh God help ye . . .'

'I'm just trying to keep the weight down . . .'

'Does the stick help?'

'It helps the balance . . .'

This is all in front of me, he thought.

But despite his age he felt good, felt ridiculously proud he had outlived his father who had died at the early age of forty-five. He didn't have a problem that would drive him to sit on a park bench with his head in his hands. So he felt good about that. He looked up at the clock above the posters. He picked up his pee pot and headed for the laboratory again.

This time when he looked away from the little machine which drew his blood he saw a crow settling in the branches of the tree outside. The thinnest of pinpricks and again she milked the blood from his finger into her glass capillary. This stranger was holding his hand. Her perfume radiated into his space – not perfume, but soap – maybe the smell of her shampoo. Camomile, maybe. She clipped her capillary to a little sloped rack. There were two of them now, like the double red line he'd had to rule beneath the title of his essays at school. He provided another urine sample.

When he sat down again in the waiting room he finished his jug of water and asked for another. He returned to his book. And as he read, the room gradually disappeared. Somewhere in southern Russia a train stopped at a small station on a May evening. The sun was setting and the station buildings threw long shadows. The student gets off to stretch his legs. He sees the stationmaster's daughter. She, too, is utterly captivating. As she stands talking to an old lady the youth remembers the Armenian's daughter, the girl with the white kerchief, and the sadness it brought him. Again he experiences the whoosh of feeling and tries to analyse it but cannot. Not only was the student, Chekhov, watching this exquisite woman, she was being watched by almost all the men on the platform, including a ginger telegraphist with a flat opaque face sitting by his apparatus in the station window. What chance for someone like him? The stationmaster's daughter wouldn't look at him twice.

He was struck yet again by the power of the word. Here he was – about to be told he had difficult changes to make to his life and yet by reading words on a page, pictures of Russia a hundred years ago come into his head. Not only that, but he can share sensations and emotions with this student character, created by a real man he never met and translated by a real woman he never met. It was so immediate, the choice of words so delicately accurate, that they blotted out the reality of the present. He ached now for the stationmaster's daughter the way the student aches. It's in his blood.

He paused and looked at the clock. It was time again. He gave another blood sample and when providing the urine sample he splashed the label. He patted it dry with toilet roll and hoped that the technician with the long hair wouldn't notice.

In the waiting room he returned to his book. Was the story accurate? About such feelings? Was this not about women as decoration? Neither woman in the story said anything – showed anything of her inner self – in order to be attractive. Was this not the worst of Hollywood before Hollywood was ever thought of? Audrey Hepburn – Julia Roberts – the stationmaster's daughter.

'There's the water you asked for.'

'Oh thanks.'

He poured himself another glass. The water was icy. With his concentration broken he looked at the posters on the wall. He could barely bring himself to read them. They made him quake for his future. But he couldn't be that bad – his doctor had referred him because he was 'borderline'. The poster warnings were for the worst cases. *Diabetic retinopathy* – can lead to permanent loss of vision. Blindness. Never to be able to read again. *Atherosclerosis* leading to *dry gangrene*. Wear well-fitting shoes, visit your chiropodist frequently. Care for your feet. Or else you'll lose them, was the implication. Jesus. He drained the glass and poured himself another.

The door, which had been silent for a while, screeched open and a wheelchair was pushed through. A woman in her seventies, wearing a dressing gown, was being pushed by a younger woman. The screeching door must lead to the wards. When they came into the waiting area it was obvious the old woman had no legs. She wore a blue cellular blanket over her lap. She was empty to the floor. The woman pushing her sat down on a chair in front of her. From their body language they were mother and daughter.

Their talk became entangled with the Chekhov and he read the same line again and again. He needed silence.

During his final visit to give blood he tried to joke with the technician about there being no more left in that finger. This time there were two crows perched on either side of the black nest. In the lavatory he noticed that his last sample was crystal clear. The water was just going through him.

He sat and finished the Chekhov. It was a wonderful story which ended with the train moving on under a darkening sky, leaving behind the stationmaster's beautiful daughter. In the departing carriage there is an air of sadness. The last image is of the figure of the guard coming through the train beginning to light the candles.

The next thing he was aware of was hearing his name called out by a male voice. He was sitting with his eyes closed, savouring the ending of the story. He stood. The doctor smiled – he was not wearing a white coat. He had a checked shirt and was distinctly overweight – straining the buttons. He led him into an office and looked up after consulting a piece of paper.

'Well I'm pleased to say you don't have diabetes. You

have something we call impaired glucose tolerance – which could well develop into diabetes. You must begin to take some avoiding action – more exercise, better diet. Talk it over with your GP. I'll write to him with these results.'

'Thank you.'

As he walked to the head of the stairs he heard the distant door screech for one last time. He will not have to come back. No need for the oil can. He went out into the November midday and across the car park. The sun was shining. He looked up at the blue sky criss-crossed with jet trails. People travelling. Going places, meeting folk. He thought of those people he had just left who daren't misplace their outpatient cards. Above him the crows made a raucous cawing. His middle finger felt tender and bruised.

He took out his mobile and phoned his wife, dabbing the keys with his thumb. He had seen her across a dance floor forty years ago and felt the wind blow across his soul.

She sounded anxious and concerned.

'Well?'

'I'm OK,' he said.

A TRUSTED NEIGHBOUR

Ben dried a fork and set it in the correct compartment of the cutlery drawer. Maureen liked to keep them all facing the same way so that they socketed together. The same with the spoons. He stared vacantly out the window at the Warners, the old couple next door. Their kitchens faced each other. They were fussing around behind swagged net curtains making their evening meal.

The girls had gone to the school disco and Ben was hopeful. Maureen was in the sitting room watching the News. He joined her at the closing music and was about to switch the television off.

'Leave that on,' she said. 'I've some ironing to do.'

Maureen went out and came back with a plastic barrel of washed clothes.

'What channel?'

'UTV.'

'Ulster television?' His voice was high with incredulity. She set up her ironing board with a clank and a metallic screech.

'It's a programme about Donegal.'

'No need to be so defensive,' he said. He went to her and kissed her, held her in his arms for a long time, caressed the D curve of her stomach – she was six months gone. The steam iron sighed as it heated.

Ben sat down. After a while he said, 'When will it be over?'

'Half past. And the answer is no.'

Ben laughed. 'You can't get *more* pregnant.'

The ironing board creaked.

'I have too much to do.'

'Like what?'

'The fact that you don't even *know* means that you have *no* idea what's involved.'

'Anything I can help with?'

'Not really.' The iron clicked against the button of a shirt. 'How's Aunt Norah?'

'Fine.'

Since her operation Ben called in most days to his Aunt's house to check on her. It was just around the corner from his work. She nearly always had a bowl of soup for him. Over his lunch he read the paper. That day in the obituary columns he'd read of the death of Dawson Orr. He hadn't told Maureen yet because such news could create uncertainty. Everything would become unpredictable and it was an extremely rare event for the two girls to be out together. He could tell her afterwards.

The programme about Donegal came on and Maureen ironed and glanced up every so often following it.

'It's lovely,' she said. 'You can nearly smell the turf smoke.'

'Do you want me to do some?'

'It's OK.'

'I can only do square things. Hankies and towels.'

'Junior Infants ironing,' Maureen said. 'I'm not going to bother doing these sheets.' She made him stand and take one end of the cotton sheet and pull it taut. Still she watched the television. They folded and pulled again and again. She advanced folding the sheet neatly. When they came together he kissed her on her averted cheek and she smiled. She made him kiss her on the mouth. 'For the look of the thing' she ironed the top and bottom of the folded sheet.

The last time Ben had seen Dawson was about a month ago. He was hardly recognisable, his face swollen up with steroids. But the moustache was there and, hidden in the pale orb of his shaved head, a distant likeness to his old self. Ben was in the Royal Victoria Hospital to visit his Aunt when a trolley with someone on it was pushed past him in the corridor. He was sure it was Dawson but the poor bastard was aware of nothing, just lolling there. The trolley turned into a private room where a uniformed RUC man stood on guard.

The other thing that stayed with him that day was the girl in the bed next-but-one to his Aunt. She was about fourteen, a child with long dark hair – very pale, very still, sitting straight up, not propped on her pillows. He asked about her. It looked like she had measles or chickenpox.

'No,' said his Aunt, lowering her voice. 'She was near that bomb in King Street.' The girl turned to look at Ben. The other side of her face was pale and without a mark.

'She knows we're talking about her,' Ben said.

'She knows nothing of the sort,' said his Aunt. 'She hasn't heard a thing since she came in here, God love her.' It was remarkable, the way her face was pocked and pitted on one side but not the other. Like blizzard snow on one side of a tree-trunk. 'That's what broken glass can do to you. Compliments of the Provos,' said his Aunt.

The reason he knew someone like Dawson was because they'd been next-door neighbours at one time. When Ben and Maureen were first married they'd lived in a small student flat off the Ormeau Road. Their family grew – two girls came in the space of three years.

'Very Roman Catholic,' the guys in the department had kidded him. The flat became too small. Maureen had saved some of her Civil Service gratuity – in those days married women had to leave – and Ben got a promotion at work. They managed to put enough together for the deposit on a red-brick semi in a mixed Catholic and Protestant area.

Several months after they moved into the house Ben discovered what his next-door neighbour, Dawson Orr, did for a living. Their two wives had swapped the information across the chicken-wire fence which separated their properties. When asked what her husband did, Mrs Orr was somewhat hesitant. She said something about the Civil Service. Maureen laughed at the coincidence and said that she, too, had worked in the Civil Service before she was married – what branch was her husband in? Reluctantly

Mrs Orr admitted, almost under her breath, that her husband was in the police.

Maureen thought her attitude entirely reasonable. She'd have done the same thing if she'd been in her shoes. The situation in Northern Ireland in those days was appalling. People being driven out of their homes by one side or the other. You wouldn't like to advertise the fact that you were even vaguely connected with the security forces. Explosions and petrol bombings, snipings, doorstep killings. But the area where they had bought their house was utterly quiet. All the trouble seemed to be happening on television.

Both neighbours had young families – the three Orr children were a year or two older than Ben's. And at that age such a difference is crucial. Their not playing together had nothing to do with them being a different religion.

Sometime after that conversation between the wives Ben and Dawson shook hands over the fence. Ben's impression was that he had just clasped a bunch of warm sausages. Dawson Orr was a big man – in middle age – between forty and fifty with a round face and double chins. He had a little moustache which he was forever touching – sometimes a stroke with his fingertips, sometimes with an upward movement of the back of his knuckle as if he was trying to shape it into handlebars.

'I'm very easygoing,' he would say. 'But don't try to put one over on me. I don't have any degrees but then you don't need them in my line of work. Because you're up against boyos as thick as two short planks. I can run rings round most people.' Then he laughed. He had a nice laugh, his face all creased and his eyes were dancing in his head.

The next morning when Ben was walking the long avenue to the bus terminus he heard the deep-throated rumble of a motorbike behind him. Dawson pulled up in the grey light.

'Want a lift?'

'What is it?'

'A Norton.'

Ben swung his leg over and sat balancing. The bike took off shakily. 'You'll have to learn to ride pillion,' Dawson shouted over his shoulder. 'Lean with the bend. Relax. Don't fight it.' Ben put his hands lightly on Dawson's back and sensed the big body beneath the clothes. When they hit the main road Dawson pretended to be a commentator with an American accent. 'And Artie Bell is going flat out – doing the full fuckin hundred down the Seven Mile Straight. Are you OK?' He had to shout to be heard. 'Try as far as possible to keep your shit internal.'

The lift didn't happen every morning but was an occasional thing. Sometimes, according to what the weather was like, Dawson wore a belted creamy gabardine, sometimes a black leather jacket. 'You can put your arms around me. Or if you don't fancy that – join your hands behind your back.' If Ben kept his eyes fixed ahead then he discovered that his body naturally adopted the correct angles. There were fat horizontal creases in Dawson's neck. He couldn't imagine putting his arms around him and yet he hadn't enough bravado to hold onto nothing. So he put his hands on Dawson's back, up near the shoulders. He thought he was aware of a ridge or strap beneath the clothing and wondered if it was a holster. Policemen carried guns, didn't they? 'Your instinct's to lean the wrong way. Remember the Wall of Death.' If they went into a corner and Dawson felt that Ben was resisting he'd laugh and shout 'The Wall of Death – fuck ya.'

Dawson never wore a uniform so Ben assumed that he must be a detective of some sort. Maybe even Special Branch. Neither did he wear a motorcycle helmet. If he was stopped by the police he would just say who he was. If it happened on a morning when Ben was on the back he hoped Dawson would get his pillion passenger off the rap as well.

Dawson also had a car, a big red Cortina parked at the side of the house. The Orrs' garage was like Smithfield market – stacked to the door with junk and abandoned toys and washing machines that no longer functioned. Ben couldn't work out when or why Dawson used which method of transport. When he drove past him in the car he never offered a lift, even if it was pouring. Then one morning Ben was just turning out of the avenue onto the main road when he saw Dawson driving the Cortina and taking a right turn – and driving out of town.

The only time Dawson visited was late at night. Usually he was a bit drunk.

He didn't ring the doorbell but just tapped the lit and curtained window with the tip of his car key. It was a small

sound but it always scared the shit out of Ben. At times like
these. Someone outside. Ben would switch on the outside
light and see the bulky figure through the full-length ribbed
glass. Then open the door.

'I see you're not in bed yet.'

'Not yet.'

Dawson lowered his shoulder and made to step in. Ben
could do nothing but swing the door open. Dawson
proceeded into the living room where Maureen smiled up
at him and turned off the television. He sat in Ben's warm
armchair by the hi-fi, the car keys still in his hand. His
leather jacket creaked when he moved.

'I'm just on my way to bed,' she said. Dawson grinned,
his eyes heavy.

'You don't wait for the Queen, then?'

'Does anybody?'

'You'd be surprised.' Dawson laughed.

Maureen lifted two empty cups and a crumb-covered
plate. Now that the television was off she lowered her voice
and looked up meaningfully at the ceiling.

'If you waken those children, I'll kill the both of you.'
Ben was sitting down. 'Don't be too long – you've your
work in the morning, Ben.'

'What about me?' said Dawson.

'Yeah, you too.'

When Maureen left the room and could be heard turning
on and off taps in the kitchen Dawson said, 'Have you any
drink in the house? Eh?'

'There's a bottle of home-made wine there. But the only reason it's there is because it tastes so awful. Elderberry.'

'No beer?'

'No. If there's drink in the house it generally gets drunk the same evening.'

Dawson reached into his pocket and produced a flat half-bottle of Bushmills. There was already some out of it.

'Do you fancy a wee Bush?'

'Aye.'

'It'll help you sleep.' Dawson held out his arms. 'A glass and some water is all we require. Civilised standards must be maintained.'

Ben went into the kitchen and Maureen raised an eyebrow to him. She was holding an empty hot-water bottle in her arms waiting for the kettle to boil.

'He's got some whiskey,' Ben whispered.

'Keep him quiet. No big laughing.' Ben got tumblers and a milk jug full of water and went back into the living room where Dawson was twisted in the chair tilting his head trying to read the spines of Ben's LPs. Ben poured and watered the whiskey.

'Cheers,' said Dawson.

'*Sláinte.*'

They clinked glasses. Dawson drank half his tumbler in one go and smacked his lips.

'A Protestant whiskey for a Protestant people,' he said. 'What kinda music are you into at the minute?'

'Miles Davis.'

71

'Who?'

'Trumpeter – jazz. Very cool.'

'Fuck that. There's nobody like the King. The greatest thing since sliced bread. There's nobody to touch him.' It was too much of an effort for Dawson to get up so he moved his pelvis in the chair a little. He began to croon the words of 'Are You Lonesome Tonight'. Ben shushed him, pointing upstairs. Dawson stopped and launched into a conspiratorial whisper.

'Sorry. Forgot myself.' He looked at the shelf beside him. 'Who likes the ceilidh music?'

'Maureen. She's a country girl.'

'Diddley-di music – that's what I call it. All very same-y. I couldn't be bothered with it. That's not a criticism. It takes all sorts, eh? We are all thrown together whether we like it or not. Gotta make the best of it. You're a nice guy.' Dawson winked at him. Ben could hardly believe it. 'It's good to have you next door. I mean it could be anybody – any Tom, Dick or Harry. Or Shaun or Seamus. If only they were all like you.'

'What are you on about?'

'You know . . . in my . . .' He shrugged his shoulders and the leather of his jacket made a sound. Was that bulge made by his gun? 'A trusted neighbour is an important thing.'

'What do you mean?'

'You could go to anybody. Shop me.'

'If that's what you think . . .' Ben stared at him.

'I don't mean you. *One's next-door neighbour.* Would be in a position . . . kinda thing.'

'Who would I shop you to?'

72

'One's friends.'

'I have no friends like that.'

'Oh I know, I know. I'm only speaking in general.' He drank off what remained in the glass. 'A word here and a word there – it might get around.' He refilled his glass. 'I see you're not ready yet.'

Ben looked at his watch and turned on the News on the radio. Another body had been found hooded and shot through the head on the Seven Mile Straight.

'Why's it always the Seven Mile Straight?' said Ben.

'You can see headlights coming from a long way off. Gives you time to take cover or tidy up. Put the finishing touches to whatever you're doing.'

The next morning Ben got a lift on the back of the bike. Neither of them spoke a word. Dawson dropped him at his work on the Lisburn Road and then sped on through the traffic, his arm raised in a wave.

Around about the time Dawson started calling late at night there was a colleague, Paul Magill, who'd come into work in a terrible state one day. He lived in a dodgy mixed area somewhere up near Alliance Avenue and he'd been threatened by Loyalists. They were going to burn him out. If not tonight, then some night soon. Their windows had already been broken twice – and somebody had fired a shot at the house, gouging a hole in the brickwork. He and his family were going to have to move – he had two wee boys. He said he was going to stay at his parents' place until they got somewhere. But in the meantime they had nowhere to put their stuff.

'I've a garage,' Ben said. 'And no car.'

That evening Paul drove up in a borrowed lorry. The open back was full of his furniture. 'When you see this stuff in the light of day . . . it seems hardly worth saving.'

There was a butcher's smell of fat and raw meat off the wood. Bloodstains were on the walls and tailgate.

'Jesus who owns the transport?'

'Charlie the hide man's. It was this or nothing.'

'I thought you'd been out murdering.'

Paul had his brother, Vincent, with him. He said, 'That's in the future.'

They unloaded everything into the garage. It had all been thrown together in great haste. Cardboard boxes full of things that shouldn't have been together. In one, cups and glasses and a yellow duck and a telephone directory. Another with saucers and fire-irons and tasselled cushions, doily mats and enamel-backed hairbrushes which were obviously family heirlooms. There were sad, intimate things like a scarlet brassiere and suspender belt which Paul, when he noticed they were on show, covered with a pillow. Sagging sofas and bicycles and bed-heads and scuffed armchairs. All three of them were needed to lift the old-fashioned, heavy bed frame with its springs which clashed and shivered when they set it down on the concrete floor.

Next door Mrs Orr came into her kitchen to do the dishes and watched the unloading. She smiled and waved.

When everything was stored in the garage Ben pulled down the door and they went into the house for a cup of tea. Maureen was very concerned for Paul. She laid her hand on his shoulder as they sat at the kitchen table.

'You poor thing,' she said. Paul nodded – agreeing with her.

'It's unbelievable,' said Vincent.

'How can it happen,' said Maureen, 'in this day and age – that the police can't protect you in your own home?'

'Because the police – as you call them – are even worse.'

'They're practically ushering the bastards through,' said Vincent, 'pointing out the Catholic houses. Can I light your petrol bomb for you, sir? May I draw your attention to number fourteen, sir – so far it's gone completely unscathed.'

'Aw come on. It's not as bad as that,' said Maureen.

'Did you not see them at Burntollet? Siding with the ones that stoned us.'

'Us?' said Maureen.

'Vincent's been on every Civil Rights march so far,' said Paul, smiling.

'They were standing around chatting up Loyalist guys wearing armbands who were openly organising the stone throwing.' Vincent's voice rose in pitch, then dropped again. 'All very lovey-dovey.'

'I don't distinguish between them any more.'

'There's bigots and bigots in uniform.'

'But every state must police itself,' Ben said. 'Law and order is important.'

'Their law . . . their idea of order . . .' Vincent snorted. 'If I knew where a cop lived . . . I swear to God I'd . . .' His fists were knotted on the table and around his mouth had become pale. 'Maybe not me but . . . He'd be dealt with. I'd make sure of it. Fuckers like that . . .'

'Careful with the language,' said Maureen. She listened to hear where the children were playing. Vincent put up his hands in admission. Ben looked at Maureen and their eyes met and held for a moment. Paul grinned.

'The family firebrand. Is it any wonder he's on the pirate radio.'

'Shut up Paul.'

'Which one?'

'Well it's not Radio Orange or the Voice of Ulster.'

'I can never find any of them on the dial,' said Maureen.

'They're jamming them all the time now.'

It was a Saturday some weeks later when Dawson and Ben coincided at their back doors. Ben was going to the garage for a hammer.

'Hi,' said Dawson. 'That's a pisser of a day.'

'Aye.' Ben bent to open the garage door. The up-and-over mechanism screeched as the door went up.

Dawson came closer to the fence and stood smiling.

'Who's is all the stuff?' He nodded into the dark garage.

'A mate at work.'

'Is he in there too?' Dawson laughed.

'Naw – he was threatened out of his house.'

'Where was he living?'

'Ardoyne.'

Dawson gave a low whistle. He came right up to the chicken-wire fence and stared into the open garage.

'How long have you to keep it for?'

'Until he gets another place.'

Dawson was trying to figure out what he was seeing.

'Filing cabinets and everything,' he said, shaking his head.

'I don't know what's in there,' said Ben.

'Are there papers and stuff?'

'Anything and everything,' said Ben. 'D'you mean newspapers?'

'Naw – documentation.'

'I've no idea what's there. I'm just doing him a favour.'

'If he's living in the Ardoyne he must be keen.'

'On what?'

'The cause.'

'What?'

'The Republican cause.'

'Get a grip. How would I know? I only work with him. It's a favour.'

'What do you call him?'

Ben hesitated.

'A big bastard – among other things.'

Dawson laughed then said, 'There wouldn't be too many from the Ardoyne who wouldn't be involved, eh Ben?'

'In what?'

'Come on, you know what I'm talking about. What do

you think? I mean that could be why they were threatening him.'

'Why?'

'He's involved.'

'Not at all.'

Ben turned his back and went into the garage. He began rooting about, looking for his toolbox. Dawson leaned his elbow on the cement post which held up the wire fencing watching him.

'The Ardoyne is a rough place right now. Indian country. You wouldn't want to be going in there after dark. Come to think of it you wouldn't want to be going in there at any time of the day or night. I mean, *you* could go. But not me.'

'I don't know it at all.' Ben was having to shout from inside the garage.

'They've arms dumps and bomb factories and pirate radio stations and God knows what.' Suddenly Dawson's voice was right beside him. He must have walked the whole way round the fence and down Ben's drive. Ben found his toolbox and knelt down in front of it. He opened the lid and pulled up the sections, which then became a staircase of trays on either side. He selected a picture hook and some nails.

'I've got one of those toolboxes too. They're very handy.' Dawson was beginning to move in amongst the stored furniture, looking at this and that.

'It's difficult to tell if people are involved. They don't grow horns or anything.'

'He's not involved. I know. The Loyalists threatened him

78

because he was . . . a Catholic – and he was sure it was going to turn into another Bombay Street . . .'

'I'll tell you one thing about Bombay Street . . .'

'What?'

'They did it themselves.'

'What?'

'The Roman Catholic families torched their own houses.'

'That is the greatest load of . . . How can you say that?'

'I wasn't there to see it but it's what I'm told. By reliable colleagues.'

'Why the fuck would anyone want to burn their own house?'

'Look at it this way. Who gains? The Protestant community gets a bad name. Everything is moved that bit closer to a United Ireland. The Republicans win no matter what way you interpret it. So the Roman Catholics were persuaded to torch their own houses so's the Protestant people would lose face.'

'Dawson, are you taking the piss?'

'I certainly am not,' he laughed.

'It's a complete paradox.'

'Is it now?'

'Yeah.'

'Is that for whitening your whites?' Dawson smiled and flicked his moustache.

'No – it's a contradiction. Something that . . .'

'Can you not take a joke, Ben. I'm only winding you up. Parazone. Oxodol. Maybe you're too young to remember.

You think I don't know? What a paradox is? You think I'm not educated?'

Ben got up off his knee and closed the toolbox.

'I'd better be getting on,' he said. He picked up his claw-hammer and stood waiting for Dawson to take the hint and leave the garage. Dawson had his hands in his jacket pockets. He bent his knees and crouched a little as if to see beneath something resting on a chest of drawers. 'These things aren't mine, Dawson.'

'I know. I know. Keep your hair on,' he laughed and turned to face the light. 'You can almost smell the gelly off them.' Ben didn't laugh but stood waiting with his free arm in the air, reaching for the handle. Dawson shuffled around some cardboard boxes and out onto the driveway. Ben pulled on the up-and-over door. It swung to the floor and shut with a resounding boom. Dawson took his hands out of his pockets and wrinkled his nose. Then he brushed up his moustache.

'Hanging pictures?' he said.

'Putting up a calendar.'

Dawson walked back to his own driveway and Ben watched him. When Dawson had returned to his back door he spoke over to Ben.

'I'm only winding you up.'

Ben went into the house.

Then something odd started to happen. At first Ben hardly noticed it. Because of his work he was always up first and would move about as quietly as he could so's not to wake the children. They slept at the front of the house with their bedroom door open. Downstairs in the kitchen he'd put on the kettle. He had a technique for the radio – turn the volume to zero then switch on, slowly making it loud enough to hear. The news was depressing. Two murders. There were houses burned in the Short Strand.

This particular morning was cold. He carried his tea into the front room and pulled the curtains. He opened the slats of the venetian blind and looked out at the small garden. There had been a heavy frost and all the plants had become grey and limp. Dawson had parked his car in front of Ben's house. The silly bastard. He comes home at all hours, probably drunk, overshoots and abandons his car on the pavement in front of my bloody house. Why does he do that?

It began to happen regularly. Late at night Dawson would park his car at a rakish angle, half on, half off the pavement at Ben's gate. Over the next couple of weeks Dawson gave him many lifts on the back of the Norton. Seated on the pillion, his eyes narrowing into the wind, Ben never thought the time was right to raise the matter of the drunken driving and the careless parking. Shouting that kind of stuff into the wind seemed somehow inappropriate. Events eventually caught up and it seemed easier to say nothing. Just forget it.

Then one Sunday morning the families coincided returning from their different churches. Mrs Orr wore a hat and carried a black bible, Dawson was in a grey suit with too flashy a tie. Their children had run off to play somewhere. Ben's family were not so formal – yet they were wearing what they themselves would describe as 'their Sunday best'. Maureen carried a black missal and the children had little white prayer books.

'Good morning,' said Mrs Orr. They all exchanged greetings and passed through their front gates. Dawson caught Ben's eye and nodded him to one side.

'So,' he said. 'We're off.'

'On holiday?'

'No – moving house.' Dawson tapped the top of the wire fencing. He smiled. 'Upgrading.'

His wife overheard him and said to Maureen, 'Yes, we're on the move again.'

'Congratulations.'

'I don't know if it's congratulations or not. Another school, new teachers.' She pulled a face and looked at Dawson.

'When?'

'This week. The furniture van's coming on Wednesday.'

'Where are you going?'

'It's not definite yet.' Mrs Orr looked down at the tarmac then up at Dawson.

'Our lives are run by bureaucrats,' he said.

'Well, wherever it is I hope things work out for you,' said Ben.

'Thanks. Thanks very much. You've been great neighbours.'

There was a little flurry of movement as they all shook hands across the waist-high fence.

'You'll be sorely missed,' said Maureen. Ben remembered the sausage impression of his first handshake with Dawson. 'How will I get to my work in the mornings?' he said.

After the Donegal programme the television was switched off. The house was strangely silent. Maureen, finished with the ironing, sat on the sofa with her feet up underneath her.
'I have a craving,' she said.
'You are not alone in this,' said Ben.
'For some tea, silly. Maybe some cheese and toast?'
'How do you feel?' he said.
She took a long time to answer. Eventually she smiled without looking at him and said, 'I feel OK now.'
Immediately he bounded to his feet and went into the kitchen. He toasted some bread and melted cheese on it and spread it with brown pickle. They smiled listening to the noise they made biting into their toast. Maureen made noises of pleasure.
Just as he finished his tea he heard footsteps outside and the click of a key in the lock.
'Shit,' Ben rolled his eyes.
'Is that you both?' Maureen called. The girls came in, very down in the mouth. Yes they had shared a taxi. But there had been trouble – burning buses and rioting – and the school had decided that everyone should go their separate ways as soon as possible. The girls were livid – what difference did time make – they'd been enjoying themselves – you could always go round the trouble. As they stomped

off to their room Maureen called, 'There's a blouse each ironed for you. And don't forget to get your things ready for the morning.'

The people who bought the Orrs' house were an older couple – in their seventies. Mr Warner was a retired bank manager and she was, as Maureen put it, 'a retired bank manager's wife'. They were not unfriendly but neither did they stop for conversations. The first time Ben and Maureen really talked to them was in the spring at a party in the Donaldsons' house across the street. The old couple were the first to arrive and they were drinking sherry when Ben and Maureen went in. Ben thought them a little dull.

People came with their carry-outs and there were greetings and handshakes. Music was put on and turned up. To continue talking to Ben, Mr Warner sat well forward in his seat and cupped his hand behind his ear. After a while the old couple began to smile constantly, then at nine o'clock they went back home across the street.

'You scared the pensioners off,' said Bill Donaldson to Ben. Ben was coming out of the kitchen pouring himself a can of Guinness, making sure the head didn't well up and overflow the glass. They stood beside the banisters.

'Have you no pint glasses?'

'This is a house not a bar. So what did you think of them?'

'They're retired – from everything. And that includes enjoying themselves.'

Bill cocked his head sideways looking up the stairs and made mock angry noises.

'Who's out of bed then? What did I tell you two?' The little Donaldson girls sat in their pyjamas on the top step, peering down at the party. They had pageboy haircuts. They were used to their father's mock angry voice because they didn't move. They smiled at Ben.

'They're doing nobody any harm,' said Ben. He shouted up, 'Sure you're not, girls.' The girls solemnly shook their heads.

'It was a shame about the Orrs having to leave,' said Bill.

'Yeah.'

'But it wouldn't have been wise for him to stay.'

'Why?'

'After the threat.'

'But all cops get threatened.'

'Not on pirate radio, they don't.' Ben stared at him. 'They gave out his address on Radio Free Whatever.'

'Fuck.'

'And the powers that be said it was a serious threat. A bomb threat. That's why he came round us all. He was very apologetic.'

'What do you mean – came round us all?'

'Didn't he come and tell you to put the girls in the back bedroom?'

'No.'

Bill looked confused.

'He said he went round everybody. Warned them.'

'Not me, he didn't.' Ben sipped at his drink and stared at Bill. 'Maybe he said something to Maureen.'

Ben went off in search of his wife. He took her from a conversation with three other women sitting on the floor and beckoned her out of the noise into a coat recess in the hall.

'Did Dawson tell you someone was itching to bomb him? Did he tell you to put the kids in the back bedroom?'

'No.'

Ben bit his lip.

'Why?' said Maureen.

'That's what I want to know. Why did he not warn *us*? He warned everybody else.'

'Jesus.'

'We're Catholics.' He threw back his head and whooped in disbelief. 'Fuckin Fenian bastards. That's what we are.'

'You don't mean it was deliberate?'

'What other way is there of looking at it?'

'Not only did he not warn us,' Ben's eyes widened with realisation, 'he tried to set us up. That's what the bad parking of the car was all about. He wasn't drunk. He didn't miss. He parked his fucking car in front of my house so's we'd get it . . .'

'Jesus. And he's got kids of his own.'

When Ben and Maureen went to bed they could hear the girls still talking.

86

They made love in silence, except for Ben's final suppressed gasp. Afterwards they made spoons. Ben put his hands on her back like he was her pillion passenger and told her that he'd seen in the paper that Dawson Orr was dead.

'Poor man,' she said. 'And that wife of his. And those poor children.' She fell asleep almost immediately. But Ben lay on his side kept awake by the image of the pale child in the Royal Victoria Hospital, sitting straight up in the bed, one side of her face peppered with wounds.

A BELFAST MEMORY

Our two rented houses faced each other across the street – my father's at seventy-three and Aunt Cissy's at fifty-four. There was another uncle, Father Barney, who used to call round most Sundays to Cissy's. In the evening they all played poker and Father Barney would drink whisky and do mock shouting and clowning. The others would roll their eyes. If the children were good and provided Father Barney wasn't 'beyond the beyonds' they were allowed to watch. My father always left early saying he had his work to go to in the morning. My mother said he just couldn't stand Uncle Barney any longer.

I knew my father's work had something to do with drawing and lettering. I'd found things in cupboards – small blocks of wood topped with grey zinc metal. If there was lettering on this metal it was always backwards, unable to be read. In cupboards there were pages of pink paper, thick as slices of bread, with lettering pressed into them and bulldog clips full of his newspaper adverts. At the moment he was illustrating a Bible for Schools. He'd shown me a drawing for the Cure at Capharnum and, as an exercise, made me read aloud the caption:

'They could not get in because the house was crowded out, even to the door. So they took the stretcher onto the roof, opened the tiles, and let the sick man down.'

I was about eight or nine at the time. It was dead easy.

It was a Sunday and felt like a Sunday. *Family Favourites* was on the wireless. My father sat beneath the window for the best light.

'What you doing?'

He held up the drawing.

'Abraham and his son, Isaac,' he said. A man with a white beard beside a boy carrying a tied-up bundle of sticks. '*"Where is the victim for the sacrifice?"* That's what the boy is saying.' My father put on a scary, deep voice and said, 'Little does he know . . .' He drew quietly for a while. The pen scratched against the paper and chinked in the ink bottle. He had a pad on the table and sometimes he made scratches on it. 'Just to get the nib going.' Sometimes the pen took up too much ink and he shook it a little. 'You're no good if you can't make something out of a blot.'

The hall door opened and footsteps came in off the street. My father stopped and looked up. It was my cousin, Brendan, who was a year and two months older than me. He was a good footballer.

'It's yourself, Brendy.'

Brendan stopped in the middle of the floor and said, 'Charlie Tully's in our house having a cup of tea.'

'Go on. Are you kidding?'

'No.'

My father gave a low whistle.

'This we will have to see.' He wiped his pen on a rag, then rinsed it in a jam jar of water. He blew on his drawing then folded the protective tissue over it.

'Come on.' All three of us went across the road. The only car parked on the street belonged to Father Barney.

'Did Barney bring him?' Brendan nodded.

'And Terry Lennon.'

Terry Lennon was a blind church organist. He had a great Lambeg drum of a belly with a waistcoat stretched tight over it. He would sit in the armchair by the fire smoking constantly, never taking the cigarette from between his lips. A lot of the time he stared up at the ceiling – his eyelids didn't quite shut and some of the whites of his eyes showed. Now and again he would run his fingers down the cigarette to dislodge the ash onto his waistcoat. Aunt Cissy called him Terry Lennon, the human ashtray.

When we went in Terry Lennon was in his usual chair. Father Barney stood in front of the fire with his hands behind him. On the sofa was a man, still wearing his rain-coat, drinking tea. His hair was parted in the middle. He was introduced to my father as Charlie Tully.

'You're welcome,' said my father. 'Is that sister of mine looking after you?'

Charlie Tully nodded.

'The best gingerbread in the northern hemisphere,' said Father Barney. 'That's what lured him here.'

'Where's the old man?' said my father.

'The last I saw of him was heading up to the lavatory with the *Independent*.'

'He'll be there for a week.' My father turned to the man in the pale raincoat.

'I bet he was delighted to see you Mr Tully – he's a bit of a fan.'

'Oh he was – he was.'

'So – how do you like Scotland?'

'It's a grand place.'

'Will Mr Tully have a cigarette?' Terry Lennon reached out in the general direction of the voice with his packet of Gallagher's Greens.

'Naw, he only smokes Gallagher's Blues,' said Aunt Cissy and everybody laughed.

'If you'll forgive me saying so Mr Tully,' said Terry Lennon, 'the football is not an interest of mine. You understand?'

'I do. You were making some sound with that organ this morning.'

'Loud ones are great.' Terry Lennon laughed. 'Or Bach. Bach is great for emptying the place for the next mass. The philistines flee.'

There was a ring at the door and Brendan went to answer it. When he came back he said it was Hugo looking for a drink of water.

'And run the tap for a while,' said Aunt Cissy laughing. 'Bring him in.'

'The more the merrier,' said my father.

'Wait till you hear this, Mr Tully. Our Hugo.' Brendan went into the kitchen and ran the tap very fast into the sink. He carried a full cup into the room and called Hugo from the door. Hugo edged into the room and accepted the cup. There was silence and everybody watched him drink. Hugo was a serious young man who was trying to grow a beard.

Father Barney joined his hands behind his back and rose on his toes. He said, 'So you like to run the tap for a while?'

'Yes, Father.'

'And why's that?'

'The pipes here are lead. And lead is poison. Not good for the brain.'

'The Romans used a lot of lead piping,' said Father Barney, winking at Charlie. 'Smart boys, the Romans. They didn't do too badly.'

'No – you're right, Father. But maybe it's what *destroyed* their Empire,' said Hugo. 'Being reared to drink poison helps no one.'

Father Barney sucked in his cheeks and rolled his eyes. 'I need a whisky after that slap down.' Aunt Cissy moved to the sideboard where the bottle was kept. 'Cissy fill her up with water, lead or no lead. Will anybody join me? What – no takers, at all?' He held up his glass. 'To Mr Tully here. God guide your golden boots.' Granda came downstairs and had to push the door open against the people inside.

93

'What am I missing?' he said.

'A drink,' said Father Barney. Granda looked around in mock amazement.

'He's getting no drink at this time of the day,' said Aunt Cissy. Granda was still wearing his dark Sunday suit and the waistcoat with his watch-chain looped across it. On his way to mass he wore a black bowler hat.

'It's getting a bit crowded in here,' Granda said, looking around the room. 'Reminds me of the day McCormack sang in our house in Antrim. There was that many in the room we had to open the windows so's the neighbours outside could hear him.'

'*Count* John McCormack?' said Charlie Tully.

'The very one.'

'How did the maestro end up in your house?'

'Oh, he was with Terry there, some organ recital.'

'And what did he sing?'

'Everything. Everything but the kitchen sink. "Down by the Sally Gardens", "I Hear You Calling Me".'

'It was some show,' said Terry Lennon, putting his head back as if listening to it again.

'Would you credit that?' said Charlie. 'I met a man who knows Count John McCormack.'

There was a strange two-note cry from the hallway: 'Yoo-hoo.'

'Corinna,' said Cissy and pulled a face. The door was pushed open and Corinna and her sister, Dinky, stood there.

'Full house the day,' said Corinna. She eased herself into the room. Dinky remained just outside.

'The house is crowded out, even to the door,' said my father.

'Is there any chance of borrowing an egg, Cissy? I'd started the baking before I checked.' Cissy went into the kitchen and came back with an egg which she handed to Corinna.

'Thanks a million. You're too good.' Corinna stood with the egg between her finger and thumb. 'What's the occasion?' She vaguely indicated the full room.

'Charlie Tully,' said Cissy. 'This is Corinna Coyle. And her sister Dinky.' Cissy pointed over heads in the direction of the front hall. Dinky went up on her toes and smiled.

'A good-looking man,' said Corinna.

'Worth eight thousand pounds in transfer fees,' said Father Barney.

'He's above rubies, Cissy. Above rubies.' And away she went with her egg and her sister.

'So,' said Granda, 'will we ever see Charlie Tully playing again on this side of the water?'

'Maybe.'

'Internationals,' said Hugo.

'But it's not the same thing,' said Granda, 'as watching a man playing week in, week out. That's the way you get the whole story.'

'There's talk of a charity game with the Belfast boys later in the year,' said Charlie.

'Belfast Celtic and Glasgow Celtic?' Granda was now leaning forward with his elbows on the table. 'There wouldn't be a foul from start to finish.'

'Where'd be the fun in that?' said Father Barney. 'Cissy, I'll have another one of those.'

Cissy went to the sideboard and refilled the glass. 'Remember you've a car to drive.'

Barney ignored her and pointed at my father. 'Johnny there would design you a programme for that game. For nothing. He's a good artist.'

'Like yourself Charlie,' said Granda.

'Is that the kinda thing you do?' Charlie said.

'Yeah sure,' said my father. Barney started mock shouting as if he was selling programmes outside the ground. Some of his whisky slopped over the rim of the glass as he waved his arms. My father smiled.

'Have you been somewhere – before here?'

'On a Sunday morning?'

Barney looked over to Charlie Tully. 'Johnny does work for every charity in the town. The YP Pools, the St Vincent de Paul, the parish, even the bloody bishop – no friend of mine – as you well know – his bloody nibs. Your Grace.' He gave a little mock inclination of the head. Cissy ordered Brendan out of his chair and told Barney to sit and not be letting the side down.

'So Charlie,' said Granda, 'the truth from the insider – is there no chance of Belfast Celtic starting up again?'

'Not that I know of.'

'We gave in far too easily. In my day when somebody gave you a hiding, you fought back.'

'Aye, it's all up when your own side makes you the scapegoat,' said Aunt Cissy.

'I mean to say,' Granda's voice went up in pitch. 'What were they thinking of?'

'The game of shame.'

'A crowd of bigots.'

'They came streaming onto that pitch like . . . like . . . bloody Indians.'

'Indians are good people,' said Hugo.

'. . . and they kicked poor Jimmy Jones half to death. Fractured his leg in five places. And him one of their own. It ended his career.'

'Take it easy, Da,' said Father Barney and slapped the arm of his chair.

'You were at the game?' said Charlie Tully.

'Aye and every other one they've ever played,' said Granda. 'I don't know what to do with myself on a Saturday afternoon now. I sometimes slip up to Cliftonville's ground but it's not the same thing. *Solitude*. It's well named.' Granda was shaking his head from side to side. 'I just do not understand it. What other bunch of people would do it? The board of directors,' he spat the words out. 'The team gets chased off the pitch, its players get kicked half to death and what do they do? OK, we're going to close down the club. That'll teach you. In the name of Jesus . . .' Granda stopped talking because he was going to cry. He looked hard at the top of the window and he kept swallowing. Again and again. Nobody else said anything. 'Why should we be the ones sacrificed? Is there no one on our side who has any guts at all?'

'Take it easy,' said my father. 'They have the sectarian poison in them.' He reached out and put his hand on Granda's shoulder. Shook him a little.

Granda recovered himself a bit and said, 'It would put you in mind of the man who got a return ticket for the bus – then he fell out with the conductor so, to get his own back, he walked home. That'll teach him.'

There were smiles at that. The room became silent.

'It was a great side,' said Charlie Tully at last. 'Kevin McAlinden, Johnny Campbell, Paddy Bonnar . . .'

'Aye.'

'And what a keeper Hugh Kelly was.'

'Aye and Bud Ahern . . .'

'Billy McMillan and Robin Lawlor.'

'Of course.'

'Jimmy Jones and Eddie McMorran and who else?'

'You've left out John Denver.'

'And the captain, Jackie Vernon.'

'And yourself, Charlie,' said Granda. 'Let's not forget yourself, maestro.'

Sometime later that year – which became known to Granda as 'the year Charlie Tully called' as opposed to 'the year McCormack sang in the house in Antrim' – I noticed drawings and sketches of my father's lying about the house. They were of players in Celtic hoops in the act of kicking or heading a ball. Their bodies were tiny cartoons but their heads were made from oval photos of the real players.

*   *   *

It was many years later – half a century, in fact – before I would remember these drawings again. My father died when I was twelve and my mother was so distraught that she threw out all his things. If she was reminded of him she would break down and weep so every scrap of paper relating to him had to be sacrificed.

Recently I was in Belfast and I wondered if there might be a copy of the programme lying around Smithfield Market. I found a small shop entirely devoted to football programmes so I went in and told them what I was looking for – a Belfast Celtic v Glasgow Celtic match programme from the early fifties.

The man looked at me and said, 'Put it this way. I'm a collector and I've never seen one.'

I was disappointed. Then he said, 'If you do catch up with it, you'll pay for it.'

'How much?' I was thinking in terms of twenty or thirty quid.

'A thousand pounds. Minimum.'

I'm not really impressed by that kind of rarity value – but in this case I thought, 'Good on you, Johnny. After all the work for charity.' If that price is accurate I don't want to own the real thing – but I wouldn't mind seeing a photocopy. A photocopy would be good. Above rubies, in fact.

THE WEDDING RING

Ellen Tierney 1884–1904

Annie Walsh, a stout woman in her early sixties, stood at the
ironing board smoothing a white pillowcase. She liked to use
two irons so that she could work continuously – smoothing
with one while the other was heating. Her sister Susan, younger
by twelve years, sat on a stool by the kitchen range with a
hanky in her hand. She had not cried for some time, but it
was at the ready because she knew she would cry again soon.

'Will you be using the goffering iron?' she asked.

'Aye – a wee touch.'

Susan put the poker between the bars into the red heart
of the fire.

'One more should finish it,' said Annie. The ironing board
creaked as she put her full weight on the material. Susan set
the next hot iron on its heel near her sister's hand. Annie
picked it up and spat the tiniest of spits onto its surface,
testing it. The moisture fizzed and danced on the black shine,
then disappeared. Annie finished the pillowcase and started
on the nightgown. When she came to the lace at the neck
she nodded for the poker. Susan tried to withdraw it from
the fire but the handle was hot, even through the handkerchief. Annie made an exasperated noise with her tongue. The

poker was red hot and when dust motes touched it they momentarily sparked white. Annie quickly inserted it into the hollow tube of the goffering iron, then grasped the moist lace in her hands and pressed it over the tube. The material made sighing noises here and there as she worked her way around it. When she was finished she held her work at arm's length.

'Ready?' Her sister sat, not saying anything. 'I could still send for Emily Mooney to help. But I feel it's something we should do ourselves. Keep it in the family.'

Annie always wore a gold cross pinned horizontally to the dark material at her throat. If she wore it the right way up the top irritated the underside of her double chin. And she was forever looking down – at her prayer book or her embroidery. Even on other people. She was taller than most and bigger in girth. Mr McDonald, the boarder who had stayed with them longest, described her as 'a ship in full sail'.

'Some soap.' Susan lifted a bar of carbolic from the wall cupboard and sawed a slice off it.

'Is that enough?'

'Remember to wash that knife – or it'll taste the bread.' Annie picked up the pillowcase and ran her hand over its surface. 'The Belfast linen looks so rich.' You could see by her eyes that she had been crying too. But she had finished and was determined not to start again.

Susan thought her sister the strongest person she knew. Everything she did, she did with determination. The knock at the door at all hours of the day and night would be for her – to bring somebody into the world or to lay somebody out. And there were times the two things happened together. Their younger sister, Elizabeth Tierney, had died giving birth to her first child, Ellie. Five years later Ellie's father had died of consumption and the two of them had reared the child as if she was one of their own. All this as well as running a boarding house for three, sometimes four gentlemen.

Annie made a pile of the sheets and pillowcases and set the soap and face-cloth on top of the nightgown. Her white apron was stiffened with starch and it created small noises in the silence as she moved about her business.

'It's all about appearances, Susan – giving the right impression.' Susan washed the bread knife then filled the ewer from the steaming kettle and set it in the basin. She looked distraught.

'Be brave,' said Annie.

'I can hardly believe we're sisters,' said Susan.

'Is that water warm enough?' Annie cupped her hand to the side of the delft but pulled it away quickly. She picked up all her paraphernalia and began climbing the narrow staircase. Susan followed her to the return room carrying the ewer and basin.

The blind was down darkening the bedroom. Susan refused to look at the bed and set the ewer and basin on the marble-topped dresser. She stood facing the wall on the edge of tears again. Annie raised the blind. The light was harsh.

'Maybe keep it down,' said Susan. 'I know nobody can see in, but . . .' Annie thought, then shrugged and pulled the blind halfway down.

'I usher them into the world and I wash them on their way out,' she said.

'But this is Ellie – family – your niece.'

'Susan – you're forgetting – it was me brought Ellie into the world.' The figure in the bed was covered by a pink satin eiderdown, which Annie herself had quilted and sewn. She took a deep breath and pulled it back.

The girl's body lay straight and to attention. A pillow supported her chin and coins weighted her eyes. Annie took them off and the lids remained closed. There was a chink as she dropped the pennies into her apron pocket. The bedclothes fell quietly to the floor. Susan put both hands to her mouth and began whispering over and over again.

'Ellie – oh wee Ellie.'

'God rest her soul.'

'I thought she was improving last night,' said Susan, 'when she got up for a while. Said it eased the pain – sitting on her hot-water bottle – God love her.'

'And when she was anointed – that helped,' said Annie. 'It was more than good of Father Logan to come out so late.'

'The doctors said there was nothing they could do.'

'The kidney man from the Mater is supposed to be the best in the world,' said Annie. 'It's amazing what they can cure nowadays. Help me lift her.'

'Where's the best place for my hands?' Annie showed her. Ellie was cold to the touch. The two women raised the body and Annie pulled the nightgown off over Ellie's head and down the stiffening arms. They carefully laid her flat again.

Susan looked shyly away from the body's whiteness and triangle of dark hair. Annie modestly covered it with a small linen towel. The material was dry and remained tented like cloth drying on a hedge.

Then Annie noticed a chain – a long chain around Ellie's neck. There was a ring on it.

'What's this?'

'I dunno.'

'A gold ring.'

'I can see that.'

'But why?'

'I know nothing about it.'

Annie turned the ring between her fingers. The fine chain holding it glittered as it moved. 'Why would anybody want to wear the likes of that? Instead of on your finger.'

'I've no idea.'

'Down her bosom?' Susan began folding the nightgown. 'A wedding ring too,' said Annie as she moved to the marble washstand to pour some hot water into the basin. She wetted and soaped a face-cloth and began washing Ellie's face, damping and pushing back the black hair from her forehead, making sure the eyes stayed closed. When she had finished the face she moved onto the body. Susan watched mesmerised by the way the skin moved, just as it would in life. The chain with the ring was in the way and Annie disentangled it and took it off over Ellie's head.

'You've never seen this before?' Annie wrinkled up her blunt nose and held up the chain.

'No. It's just a ring – all girls love to have rings.'

'But a wedding ring?'

'Especially a wedding ring.'

'Ellie could never have afforded this. You know how much one of these costs?'

Susan shook her head. No, she didn't. Sadly.

Annie was about to hang it on the bedpost when she paused.

'There's writing here. Inside. I can't make it out. It's too small. Susan, away and get me my specs.'

Susan left the room and creaked down the stairs. It was only recently that she'd needed glasses herself. Before that her eyesight had been good but now, definitely, she needed them for close work like darning or for reading a newspaper. Annie despite being so much older claimed she'd no use for them.

'Good light is all you need,' she said. 'You wouldn't miss much if you never read a newspaper. You have your eyes wore out, Susan.'

On the rare occasion she did need to see fine print she'd resort to a lorgnette which she kept in the drawer of the bureau bookcase. Susan, now with the lorgnette in her hand, climbed the staircase slowly as if it was the highest and longest staircase in the world. She knew what was coming and was filled with dread.

Susan passed the ring to her sister. Annie brought the lorgnette to her nose and focused on the inscription. 'For Ellie – *my love* – *and* – I can't make out whether that's *life* or *wife*.' Annie moved closer to the window and held it lower to catch the light coming beneath the blind. 'What do you think?' She passed the ring to Susan who read it off almost without looking.

'*For Ellie – my love and life.*'

'In the name of God . . .' Annie stared at Susan perplexed. Susan handed the ring and its chain back. Annie hung it on the bedpost again.

'What's going on here?'

'How should I know?'

'Who would have given that to her – and her only twenty? Susan, why aren't you looking at me?' Susan raised her head and looked at her sister. 'You haven't been able to meet my eye since we came up here. What's wrong with you?'

'My wee niece has just died.'

'There's something else.'

'You're wrong. There's nothing.'

'I know you of old, Susan. You think I don't know when I'm not being told the whole story?' Susan's eyes went down again and she began to weep with her whole face. Eyes, mouth, chin, the wings of her nose. She did not wipe away the tears or knuckle her eyes. While her sister cried Annie continued to wash the body. Every so often she looked up to see if her sister had stopped. Eventually she did.

Annie dried where she had washed. She said, 'Nothing unclean can enter the kingdom of heaven.' She lifted the white freshly ironed nightgown. 'Let's get this poor girl respectable again.' Susan helped Annie insert Ellie into it.

'That was a favourite of hers,' said Susan, 'with its wee ruff of lace.'

'Where's her rosary?'

It was kept in the drawer at the bedside. Susan produced a purse. In it, dark knotty beads – and Annie bound Ellie's dead and waxy hands in an attitude of prayer.

'What I want to know is,' Annie looked up, straight at Susan, 'if Ellie couldn't afford a solid gold ring, then who on earth bought it for her. And put such writing in it?'

*　　*　　*

Ellie could carry three plates at a time – one in each hand and the third balanced between her forearm and the first plate. She swooped in and set a plate before each man. Mr McDonald, a whisky traveller from Elgin in Scotland, Mr Rinforzi a string player of Italian extraction from London, and a Mr Burns from Enniskillen who worked as a clerk on the railways. Mr Burns, in his mid-twenties, was their most recent boarder. At some point during the meal Annie always came into the room having taken off her apron and positioned herself with her back to the mantelpiece.

'Is everything to your pleasement, gentlemen?' They nodded, muttering little appreciations and continuing to spoon hot soup. In the few months he'd been eating with them Annie had noticed Mr Burns's habit of bringing the cutlery, either spoon or fork, into contact with his teeth. Each time it produced a metallic wet sound. She'd remarked to Susan that Mr Burns wouldn't be used to such accoutrements at home. Where he was from, the food came in handfuls.

Ellie dashed in to set more bread on the table. Mr McDonald had finished his soup and sat with folded arms.

Mr Rinforzi was saying that he was a freethinker and that the only reason he went to mass was to hear the wonderful Carl Hardebeck play the organ.

'May God forgive you,' said Annie.

'He was one of the bishop's better appointments,' said Mr McDonald.

'The good Dr Henry Henry?' chuckled Mr Rinforzi.

'His mother suffered from double vision,' said Mr Burns. He laughed a little at his own joke and offered his empty dish to Ellie. When her fingers came in contact with it she winced and gave a little gasp. She put a finger into her mouth.

'What's wrong?' asked Mr Burns.

'A skelf. I got it earlier – out the back,' said Ellie.

'Let me have a look.'

'It's nothing,' she said and dashed out of the room.

'Such familiarity only embarrasses the lassie,' said Mr McDonald.

'Never a truer word,' said Annie, almost under her breath.

When he had finished his meal Mr Burns got to his feet and pushed back his chair with his legs.

'Excuse me,' he said with some gravity. 'But I will be back.' In his absence Annie sat upright on the edge of one of the dining room chairs. She spoke quietly to Mr Rinforzi.

'Such talk of *freethinkers* is all very well between you and me but I'd appreciate it if you'd be more circumspect when younger ears are present.'

Before Mr Rinforzi could say anything Mr Burns

returned with a small leather case in one hand and a magnifying glass in the other. Ellie was beginning to clear the table.

'We have all the equipment necessary, Miss Ellie,' said Mr Burns, 'to build the pyramids or take a mote from the eye of a gnat.'

'You'll not lay a finger on me,' said Ellie, laughing. She bunched her fists and held her elbows tightly in to her waist.

'Dr Burns at your service, ma'am.' He held the magnifying glass at some distance from his eye and regarded Ellie. The enlarged image of his eye made her laugh.

'That's horrible,' she said.

'Show me your pain.' Ellie smiled a bit. Then unfurled her middle finger. It was a cold night outside and the curtains had been drawn early to keep the heat in. 'Light,' said Mr Burns and moved her to the armchair beneath the Tilley lamp. He knelt before her, took the finger in his hand and examined it through his magnifying glass.

'I will draw the sting with my tweezers.' Ellie gave a sharp intake of breath when he touched the sensitive place.

'Do you know the story of St Jerome?' said Mr McDonald.

'Indeed you have me there,' said Mr Burns without looking up from his task.

'The lion with the limp,' said Mr McDonald. 'The saint saw what the problem was right away – a common or garden thorn. So he removed it and from that day onwards didn't the lion follow him about like a dog. Any picture of St

Jerome – look in the background and you'll see our friend the lion.'

Ellie was tightening her mouth as Mr Burns worked at her finger.

'I'm sorry but I have to go against the grain,' said Mr Burns, 'to loosen it. Could someone hold the magnifying glass for me.' Annie was reluctant to move, to have any part in this performance. Mr Rinforzi obliged.

'Going against the grain may well get you frowned upon in this house,' said Mr Rinforzi glancing at Annie. But she was looking away from the tableau. Mr Burns cradled Ellie's hand in his and brought the tweezers close. Ellie closed her eyes and then yelped.

'There we are,' said Mr Burns. He felt he had to placate Annie and laid the skelf on the white tablecloth in front of her. She declined to look down.

'Small enough to be almost invisible,' said Mr McDonald. 'Large enough to cause considerable pain.'

'Like your whisky,' said Mr Rinforzi.

Ellie was sucking the bead of blood released from her finger. Mr Burns knelt on the floor putting the things back into his case.

'I'll send you my fee, Miss Tierney,' he said.

In the kitchen Susan, flushed with heat and work, had begun to stack dishes on the draining board. Annie came in and stood with her back to the range. Her fists were rolled into a ball and she was shaking her head.

'What's getting your goat?' asked Susan.

'Ohhh.' Annie refused to answer, keeping what she had, pent up. Ellie came in with some dirty plates.

'Make sure that door is closed,' hissed Annie. Ellie backed against it and it snapped shut. 'Have you taken leave of your senses, girl?'

'What?'

'That carry-on out there. Do you know how that looks? In front of rank strangers?'

'They're not strangers. They're our boarders.'

'They're not family and never will be. They are three gentlemen who are here as paying guests, and for you to be parading around – flaunting yourself . . .' Annie mimicked what she thought was Ellie's voice. '"*Oh I've got a sore finger. Mr Burns would you like to hold my hand. Kiss it and make it better.*" I will not tolerate this . . . this sluttishness. If I see this kind of behaviour again from you Ellie I'll . . . I'll . . . You're not fit to be in the company of gentlemen.' Annie stormed out of the room and they could hear the carpeted stomps of her footsteps all the way up to her room.

Ellie stared at her Aunt Susan and her chin began to wobble. Then the tears came. Susan went to her, put her arms around her and whispered, 'She's in bad twist tonight. I could see it from early on.'

It was now much colder in the evenings and Ellie was lighting the fire in the dining room to have it warmed up in time for the evening meal. In the kitchen Susan was preparing a pie, cooking meat, chopping vegetables, rolling out pastry. Suddenly the door of the kitchen burst open and Annie strode in with her face like a clenched fist.

'What's wrong with you?' said Susan. Annie closed the door with a firm snap, made no reply and began pacing up and down. Her face was pale and her mouth drawn tight. She was arranging something inside her head.

'Has anything happened?'

Annie reached the pantry door and turned on her heel and walked back again. She looked as if she was rehearsing something – thinking through a game of draughts. Reliving old moves, anticipating new ones. Her index finger pointing things out.

'In the name of God answer me,' said Susan.

'I don't know whether I could. Or should.' Her voice was quiet, whispered, controlled. She now moved her head in the same way as she had moved her finger. Weighing, balancing, planning. She stopped pacing and put her face in her hands and remained like that for some time.

'I'm waiting,' said Susan. She was holding her chopping knife point up.

'About half an hour ago I sent Ellie to light the fire . . .' She stopped, realising this was the wrong way to begin. She began again.

'I have just seen . . . our Ellie . . . throwing herself at Mr Burns.'

'What?'

'Kissing him.' Annie almost shouted the words. Susan

covered her mouth with her hand and widened her eyes. Annie began her pacing again. 'I have said or done nothing about it – because she didn't see me. Nor did he. His back was to me. She – she was so swept away, she had her eyes closed. I was in the hall – the door was open. Her eyes closed, I tell you. Her hands were that black with the coals, she was afraid to touch him – holding them up like this, she was. Not to spoil his jacket.' Annie demonstrated as if she were trying to stop someone in their tracks. 'That charlatan of a showman – Mr Burns – he's blotted his copybook well and truly this time.'

'Maybe they're . . . they . . .' said Susan. She set her knife down on the chopping board.

'Maybe nothing,' said Annie. 'Men are only out for what they can get. Not one of them's any good – every one of them's after foulness and filth.'

'Och Annie, give us peace,' said Susan.

'And if it isn't foulness and filth they're after, it's a round-about way to lead up to foulness and filth. How dare he? I am going to ask that degenerate to pack his bags and leave *before* dinner. Him and his foul tongue. And foul ways. Did I tell you what he said at dinner last week?'

'No.'

'He didn't know I was coming into the room and he mocked your Brussels sprouts – *brothel sprouts* he called them. *Because that's what a brothel smells like,* says he. How does *he* know the smell of a brothel? And boasting about it too, into the bargain. That man makes me want to be sick.'

'Don't get yourself in such a state,' said Susan. 'You're too hard on them. They're only young. You see badness where nothing bad was meant.'

Annie sprang forward and flung the door open. She yelled at the top of her voice. 'Mr Burns! I want to speak to you right this minute. Mr Burns! And you too, Miss Ellie!'

After mass the crowds streamed out of the zinc Church of the Holy Family into the sunshine. From inside the organ boomed and warbled faintly. A parishioner stood on the steps holding a collection box for the poor. Aunt Susan and Ellie slotted some coins into it as they came down the steps into the chapel yard. They met Emily Mooney and chatted a bit. Ellie looked this way and that.

'And how's Annie?' said Emily Mooney.

'Fine. In the best of spirits. It's my week for this mass – otherwise you'd be talking to herself.'

'Give her my regards.' And she was away.

Ellie turned to Susan. 'Can I go and talk to Frank?'

'Who's Frank?'

'Mr Burns.'

'Oh, aren't we very friendly.'

'Och – Aunt Susan.'

'I'm sure Aunt Annie wouldn't . . .'

But before she had finished her sentence Ellie was away across the yard. Mr Burns, wearing a handsome Norfolk jacket, was standing by himself smoking a cigarette. He looked pleased to see Ellie, and touched his cap politely when she came up to him. They talked a little and Susan could see they were shy of each other because they moved a lot and laughed a lot. Ellie constantly fiddled with the drawstring of the little bag she carried on her wrist. Susan looked around to see if people had noticed the young couple. She strolled up and down, her hands joined at her waist. Inside the church the organ fell silent. Mr Rinforzi came down the steps, smiled and raised his hat to her in passing.

'Mr Hardebeck pulled out all the stops this morning, eh?'

The next thing Ellie was by Susan's side.

'Can we go home through Alexandra Park – with Frank?'

'But that would take ages,' said Susan.

'Yes.' Ellie smiled.

'Aunt Annie wouldn't be too pleased.'

'Please, Aunt Susan.'

'As long as you both walk with me.'

'Thank you, thank you.'

They walked down through the Limestone Road entrance to the park with Susan in the middle. To their left was the pond penned in behind waist-high railings. Swans moved quietly, looping their necks down into the water to feed, whereas the mallards and other ducks created an uproar of quacking and splashing. Mr Burns smiled and said, 'Acrimony among the duckery.' Ellie laughed.

Susan said, 'You do use such words, Mr Burns.'

'He makes them up,' said Ellie.

'Where do rooks live?' said Mr Burns defensively. All three smiled.

'Where do *you* live now, Mr Burns?' asked Susan.

'Got a good place now,' he said. Then quickly added, 'Not that there was anything wrong with my last place. I'm in the first house in Kansas Avenue. In every sense of the word.' They were strolling now – diverting to look at this bush or that flower-bed.

At one point Mr Burns said, 'Have you ever had a job, Ellie?'

'What do you call what I do? I'm never off the go – from morning till night – so's the likes of you can live like a lord.'

'That's family. What about a job – outside?'

'For a time she worked in Robb & Wylie's,' said Susan.

'Millinery,' Ellie added in a mock posh voice.

'So you know about hats.'

'I know *everything* there is to know about hats.'

'Why did you give it up?'

'They gave *me* up.'

'She was ill too often for their liking,' said Susan.

'You poor thing.'

'Ellie has to watch herself. She doesn't have a strong constitution.'

'I do so,' said Ellie. She pouted a little. 'How could I work the hours I do – lighting fires, cleaning, making beds, serving table, doing dishes? From morning till night? Maybe they discovered I was a Catholic – that would get you thrown out of a place like Robb & Wylie's much quicker.'

'They'd know what you were from the minute you walked into the shop,' said Frank. 'It's your halo that gives it away.'

Susan performed what she took to be a kindness for Ellie when she stopped at the board displaying the by-laws. The two young ones strolled on and Susan stood reading the multiplicity of 'Do Nots'. When she caught up with them again they were sitting on the grass, face to face.

'Come along, Miss Ellie – there's work to be done.'

On the way home Susan tried to reason with Ellie.

'I think he's unsuitable.'

'You make him sound like a job. I just love *him*. He's tender to me. I find him dear. And gallant. And sometimes he can be very funny.'

'Ellie you must remember that you are only nineteen.'

'How can I forget it when everybody always tells me.'

If the weather was fine this walk became a regular occurrence. On the Sundays when Ellie accompanied her Aunt Annie to the same mass they walked home by the quickest route. But with Susan the digression they took through Alexandra Park became a pleasure. Sometimes a uniformed band would be playing in the bandstand and they all sat and listened to the music.

When they arrived home Annie would ask, 'What kept you?'

Susan admitted to walking with Ellie. 'It's good for her constitution,' she said. But Susan made no mention of Frank Burns.

There was one weekend when Ellie was ill with her waterworks. Cramps and pains so bad she had to take to her bed with a hot-water bottle. After mass Susan felt obliged to seek out Frank Burns and tell him that Ellie was indisposed.

On another occasion – after Susan had sat on a park bench for a considerable time as the two young ones strolled the perimeter of the park – she and Ellie were returning home by the Antrim Road.

'He seems so ardent,' Susan said.

'What's ardent?'

'Keen.'

'Yes, he's keen,' and Ellie smiled widely and swirled around so that her dress flared out at her ankles. 'Can you keep a secret?' Susan nodded unsurely. 'He asked me to marry him.'

'Oh child dear,' Susan clapped her hand to her heart and rolled her eyes. 'In the name of God. Ellie you *must* say no. Aunt Annie would have a fit. She'd kill the both of us. *And Mr Burns.* Promise me you'll say no.'

*　　*　　*

The two sisters faced each other across the body. Annie lifted the chain and ring from the bedpost. She spilled it from one hand to the other with a little metallic hiss. She continued to stare straight at Susan.

Eventually Susan said, 'How would I know who bought it for her?'

'All the times you were out together – she never gave you the slightest hint?'

'No.' Susan shook her head. 'Did she give *you* the slightest hint when *you* were together?'

'No. But as you say – we're very different. Ellie was your pet. She would confide more in you than me.'

'I don't know,' Susan wept. 'She got days off. How do I know where she went – or who she went with?'

'So she *did* go with somebody? Who? If you were to guess, Susan, *who* would you guess?'

Still Annie changed the chain from hand to hand. Susan stared down at the pink satin eiderdown on the floor.

'You are not going to like this,' she said. 'But I would guess Mr Burns. I know you despise him but . . . she was very fond of him.'

'I might have known,' Annie almost spat the words out. 'The one and only lodger I ever had to put out. I couldn't stand to be under the same roof one more night after that display of behaviour.'

'It was only a kiss.'

'She had her eyes closed. And for all I know, so had he. She would go for the likes of him because she *knew* it would annoy me. The most unsuitable man she could think of.'

'It wasn't like that.'

'So you know what it was like. How might I ask?'

'They were very fond of each other. Maybe more than fond.' Susan returned her sister's stare. She admitted that, after Frank Burns had been sent packing, the young ones had met in her company. Other times – they might've met by themselves, for all she knew.

'So he didn't move away.'

'He's in Kansas Avenue.'

'And you stood by and watched this pair?' Annie's voice rose in pitch.

'Yes. But not all the time. Maybe they *were* married, who knows – she talked enough about it – maybe they found a priest who did it for them. Mr Burns knew a curate in St Patrick's from his own part of the country. There's no give with you, Annie. The girl's dead.'

'Did she ever tell you she was married?'

Susan nodded her head.

'Sort of.'

'And you didn't tell me.' She dropped the chain and the ring onto the linen of the bed and buried her face in her hands. Then she took her hands away from her face and said, 'Susan you're a fool. An utter and complete fool. Poor Ellie's immortal soul . . . all because of your foolishness.'

'Yesterday – she only told me this yesterday – when she felt so ill she thought she was going to die.'

'She was a good judge of one thing, at least.'

'She said she wished she'd been really married.' Susan shook her head sadly. 'Maybe they weren't married – maybe they had only plighted their troth or something – maybe they were only playing at being married, playing at being man and wife.'

Annie stared at her sister and shook her head almost in disbelief. She said, 'Susan will you go down and get me a pair of scissors. The wee nail scissors.' Susan stared back at her, then did as she was told. She left the room and went down the creaking stairway. Annie shouted after her, 'They're in the sewing basket, I think.'

Susan went to the sideboard, crouched and found the pannier where the sewing and embroidery things were kept. She had to scrabble about hunting for the scissors. There was a green pincushion bristling with needles. Tiny hanks of embroidery threads in all the colours of the rainbow. Spools of white thread. Eventually at the bottom she saw what she was looking for. She trudged back up to the return room still on the verge of tears. She handed the scissors to Annie.

'She wasn't married. Not truly,' said Annie. There was a change in her voice. It had lost its note of worry.

'How can you be so sure?'

'I checked. Just now. For my own peace of mind.'

'You checked what?'

Annie said nothing but began to clean under Ellie's nails with the point of the tiny scissors. Then she gave her sister a look.

'Jesus Mary and Joseph,' said Susan.

The weather was unseasonable for the middle of June. Susan had to hold her hat on her head or the wind would have whipped it, hatpin and all, as she struggled up the Antrim Road towards Kansas Avenue. In her other hand was the small leather purse Ellie had used for her rosary beads. In it now was the gold ring and its chain – in her mouth, terrible tidings for Frank Burns.

THE ASSESSMENT

They're watching me. I'm not sure how – but they're watching me. Making a note of any mistakes. Even first thing in the morning, sitting on the bed half dressed, one leg out of my tights. Or buttoning things up badly. Right button, wrong buttonhole. Or putting the wrong shoes on the wrong feet. I don't think there's a camera or anything, but I just can't be sure. I know computers can do amazing things because Christopher tells me they can. It's his work, and good work by all accounts. He has a new car practically every time he comes home. Or he hires a new one. He's very good – comes home a lot – never misses. And sends cards all the time. Mother's Day. Birthday. Christmas and Easter. Mother's Day.

The nurses ask questions all the time – quiz you about this and that, but I don't know which are the important things. Some of them are just chat but mixed in with the chat might be hard ones.

'Did you enjoy your tea Mrs Quinn?' Any fool can answer that but 'How long have you had those shoes?' might be a horse of a different colour. Or 'Where did you buy that brooch?'

'It's marcasite. My son bought it for me. Look at the way it glitters.'

You wouldn't know what they could take from your answer. Before I came in here they wanted to know who the Taoiseach was and I told them I'd be more interested in finding out what the Taoiseach was. Then they realised I was from the North. Somebody out of place. I told them I took no interest in politics. My only real concern is . . .

Christopher would have something sarcastic to say. 'Mother, don't be such a fool – you'll be in there to see if you can still cope living on your own. A week, two weeks at the most. They'll just keep you under observation. Surely you've heard that. *She's in hospital and they're keeping her under observation.*'

'Don't mock me Christopher.'

I have every present Christopher ever bought me. I cherish them all – mostly for his thoughtfulness. I imagine him somewhere else, in some airport or city, trying to choose something I'd like. And I look after them. Dusting and rearranging. Remembering the occasion – Mother's Day or birthday, Easter and Christmas. A cut-glass rabbit, Waterford tumblers, leaded crystal vases. When the sunlight hits that china cabinet it's my pride and joy. Tokens of affection. Things you can point to that say . . .

I don't want to be a nuisance. That's the last thing I want to be. So I make myself useful. Looking after the old people in here. The rest of them just sit sleeping – in rows – I couldn't do that – I have to be doing.

It's such a strange thing to go to bed on the ground floor, at street level almost – although my room faces out to a courtyard at the back. All my life I've slept upstairs. Feel that somebody'll be staring in at me every morning when I open the curtains. Some gardener or janitor. Getting a peep. Giving you a fright. Maybe that's part of the watching – keeping me on the ground floor. If they find out something I'd like to be the first to know. Let me in on what . . .

I don't like this room. You can't lock the door. They say no locked doors. Anybody can come in. And has.

I'm glad I like Daniel O'Donnell because they play his songs all day long. After a while you don't hear them. In the TV room all the women sit in rows and sleep – me among them. A man hairdresser comes in to do everybody's hair and if you heard him – I say a man but he has this pansy voice. But everybody likes him. There's something about him that reminds me of Christopher – the way he turns. But Christopher's voice is all right. His voice is fine.

If there was a camera I think I'd notice. But I wouldn't notice a microphone – they can hide them where you'd never find them. They could be listening. Waiting for me to talk to myself. Mutter, mutter. So I'd better not. I'll not open my cheeper for as long as I'm in here. Maybe they've got something nowadays to know what you're thinking. I wouldn't put it past them. Holy Mother of God, the thought of it. They wouldn't be able to make head nor tail of what I'm thinking . . .

But they are watching me. Making a note of any mistakes. Half dressing myself. Or buttoning up something wrongly. Or putting the wrong shoes on the wrong feet. An old woman used to visit Mammy and the tops of her stockings fell down – like a fisherman's waders. That'll be me soon enough. A laughing stock. Nobody has enough courage nowadays to . . .

There are no rules here. Just get up when you like. Eat when you like. Sleep when you like. Christopher was a terrible riser – when he came home from university in England. He'd lie till one o'clock in the day sometimes. But he passed all his exams with very high marks. First-class honours. Must have been studying in his sleep.

The problem here is I don't know what you have to do to pass. Or what will fail me. So I'm stymied. It's like going into the kitchen and saying why did I come in here. So you just drink a glass of water whether you want it or not and forget about it. Or think . . .

The question is – what'll happen? If I pass I can go home and look after myself for a while longer. If I fail . . .

In here it's like an hotel instead of a hospital – with waiters, not nurses. There's a terrible tendency for the men nurses to grow wee black moustaches. I hate them. Always did. I said to Christopher if you ever grow a moustache, you needn't bother coming home again. But moustaches or no moustaches they're watching me and taking note of any mistakes.

My favourite is Gerard – he has suddenly appeared in front of me – a nice open face. He's kindness itself. It's funny that – to be thinking of someone and they just appear. Sometimes I think there's more . . .

'You wouldn't grow a moustache – sure you wouldn't, Gerard?'

'No chance, Mrs Quinn. I tried to grow a beard once and my mother said I was like a goat looking through a hedge.'

'Promise me you'll never do it again.'

'I promise. Now could you lift up a bit and I'll get this other leg sorted. And then we'll get the tablets into you.'

'You're very good, Gerard.'

'Once the tights are on and secured, Mrs Quinn, you can face anything or anybody.' His name is in big print pinned to the lapel of his white housecoat. He pours me some water and hands me my medication on a tray – three different-coloured capsules. I take them and swallow them down with the water. He smiles.

'Thank you. How long have I been in here Gerard?'

'Six weeks. But doesn't time fly when you're enjoying yourself.'

'If you find anything out I'd like to be the first to know.'

Old age is something you never get better of. I don't seem to have as many blemishes on my face as I used to. But maybe that's because my sight is failing. Like everything else. It's like on television when you find out that the head of the police is really the baddie. And you've told him everything. Where does that leave you, eh? That must be the worst feeling in the world – when you think somebody is on your side and he turns out to be on the other side. Like a penny bap in the window – you've no say in anything. What use is a bap in the window when all's said and done? Precious little . . .

*

Christopher must be very good at his job. It's thanks to him I'm in here. He moved heaven and earth to get me a place. They're few and far between in Dublin, so I'm told. Maybe if you refuse to answer any of the questions you'll pass. The only people who'll succeed are the ones strong enough to refuse to take part. But that's not me.

This is a strange place. The patients are all doolally except me. I'm the only one in here with any common sense. In the North it's called gumption. Down here it's in short supply. There's a notice on the front door which says it must be kept shut 'as residents may wander'. In more ways than one.

They don't like us Northerners. From the day and hour I moved here I sensed it. It's as plain as the nose on your face. They couldn't give a damn. The Troubles – that's something that happens north of the Border. Nothing to do with us.

And I hate the way they talk. Like honey dripping. Smarm and wheedle – like they can't do enough for you, like you're the Queen of the May – and all the time they're ready to stab you if it suits them. Probably when your back's turned. It's why that wee Gerard is my favourite – he's from the North. I feel at home with him. Comes from Derry. He doesn't smarm and wheedle like the rest of them. I never could stand that Terry Wogan – I don't know what anybody sees in him. He should have stayed in the bank.

I'd never have come south if it hadn't been for Vincent. He was from Galway, a different kettle of fish entirely. But his job was here in Dublin. And I was his wife.

*

Yesterday I was going to the toilet and I heard knocking. There was a glass door at the end of the passage and a woman was standing on the other side of it with her hat and coat on. She had one hand flat to the window and she was rapping the glass with the ring on her other hand. Tip-tip-tip. And she was shouting but I couldn't make out what she wanted. I could see her mouth and I thought she was saying let me out. I tried the door but it wouldn't budge. There were three or four other people standing behind her, standing there like Brown's cows – queuing, as it were. So I went and got one of the nurses, the one without a moustache – and says I to him – there's people wanting out down there and I pointed. He says, 'That's OK Mrs Quinn. That's just the special unit. Take no heed of them, God love them. They're being assessed for specialist treatment.'

'I'd prefer it if you called me Cassie.'

The next time I went to the toilet they were still there, the one with her hat and coat on, tapping the glass with her ring finger. Tip-tip-tip. Sometimes in here I want to cry but crying might lose you marks. So I don't.

They've done something to my ears. The time they removed the rodent ulcer from the side of my eye – just a local anaesthetic. But in the process they did something with my ears. They've never been right since. Black and as hard as bricks. And what's more it feels like they've put them on backwards.

My name is on my door to remind me which room is mine. It's very confusing when you come into a new place like this. Corridors with doors that all look the same. Like a ship. You think you're going into your room and it's a store cupboard or a toilet. That's the kind of thing they're watching out for. But Mrs Cassie Quinn in big letters on a wee square of paper pinned to my door – that helps.

I never did a test before. An exam. Except maybe for the Catechism. You had to learn it off by heart before you could make your first Holy Communion. And that wasn't today nor yesterday. I can still mind it.

'Who made the world?'

'God made the world.'

Or Oranges Academy. To do shorthand. And typing. But it didn't really feel like an exam – you knew what you could do, give or take a word or two, before you went in. You'd be a wee bit nervous in front of your machine – maybe one or two of the keys would stick. Or you'd go deaf. Or you would suddenly freeze up. My best was seventy-five words a minute. But I'm out of the way of it now. The fingers would never cope. Two words a minute, more like. And oul Mr Carragher teaching and talking and dictating away for all he was worth with cuckoo spit at the sides of his mouth. I'm too old for tests. Or maybe I'm just too old to pass them.

The peas they gave us for dinner last night were so hard you could have fired them at the Germans.

I suppose before our first Holy Communion was a test. Father McKeown came into our school and asked us the Penny Catechism. And woe betide you if you didn't answer up, loud and clear. Who made the world? God made the world. Very good. And who is God? You, yes you at the back. God is the creator and sovereign Lord of all things . . . Everybody laughed when he asked Hugh Cuddihy what do we swallow at the altar rails when we go to Communion and he said fish. But Father McKeown was furious. Shouting at us for not being able to tell right from wrong, silly from serious. I kept very still hoping Father McKeown wouldn't see me, wouldn't ask me a question. But he did. You, you – him pointing at me – how many persons are there in God? Three persons, Father, the Father, Son and Holy Ghost. Very good. Next? I remember I couldn't stop smiling. Very good, says he. To me. Very good.

It's funny how I remember all this from long ago but nothing from this morning.

'When did your husband pass away?' Gerard asks.

'Vincent died in nineteen fifty-four.'

'That's forty-seven years ago.'

'As long as that? Seems like yesterday. Vincent was the best husband and father that ever there was. The only thing – he was always very demanding. But he was a joker as well.'

'In what way?'

'If we'd a fallout he'd bring me a bunch of weeds from the front garden. Dandelions.'

Christopher said I was becoming very forgetful. Forgetting to eat. Forgetting to get up in the mornings. Forgetting to turn off a ring on the cooker and it blasting away all night. Just as well it wasn't gas, he said. All I could do was stare down at my shoes and him at the other end of the phone. Serves me right for telling him. I'd lost weight and it was nice to see he was worried about me. My next-door neighbour,

Mrs Mallon, had phoned him, it seems. I was away to nothing. I wasn't eating. Wasn't looking after myself.

That's why they're watching me. Asking me all these questions. Making a note of any mistakes. Dressing myself like a doolally – maybe coming out of the toilet with your skirt tucked into your pants. Buttoning things up wrongly. Or putting on the wrong shoes. Looking out of place. Poor Emily McGoldrick used to visit us when she was old and the tops of her stockings fell down – like a fisherman's waders. We'd've got a clip round the ear if we'd made any remarks. Mammy was like that. Never let the side down.

I don't like this room. You can't lock the door. Anybody can come in. And did. One morning an old man in his dressing gown came in and started washing himself in my sink. I just stayed under the bedclothes. Didn't put my neb out till he'd gone. God knows what he was washing. I didn't dare look. Rummaging in his pyjama trousers and splashing and clearing his throat.

My only son, Christopher, wouldn't let me down. He's very good to me – he comes home a lot – never misses. Every November the car pulls up and he steps out of it smiling like a basket of chips. Just him – straight from the airport. Since I came in here he's taken to holding my hand like I'm his girlfriend. And he sends flowers at every turn-round. I call him my only son but that's not strictly true. I had a boy before Christopher – Eugene Anthony – but he died after three days. Not a day of my life goes past without me thinking

of him at some stage or other. The wee scrap. A doctor told
me later that he died for the want of something very simple.
A Bengal light. They discovered that years afterwards. A
Bengal light could have saved him, some way or other – don't
ask me how . . . And that only made it worse, knowing that.
I knew very little at the time – I wasn't much more than a
girl. Lying in the hospital with my bump like some class of
a fool. A baby started crying somewhere and I said is that
my baby? I hadn't a clue. Not a clue of a clue kind. Sometimes
I blame myself for wee Eugene. God love him. I think I was
nineteen at the time. But I was well and truly married.

'Tablets.'

'It it that time already, Gerard?'

'Your son'll soon be here.'

'What! How do you know?'

'He phoned. Last night. I told you, Cassie.'

'You did not.'

'I did.'

'Do you not think I'd remember something as important
as that.'

'Here's a wee sup of water to wash them down.'

'I'd better tidy myself, if that's the case.'

Gerard opens the door and shows a man in. I swear to you
I didn't know who it was.

'Christopher, what a delightful surprise.'

Aw – the hugs and kisses. He's very affectionate – kisses
me on both cheeks. In front of all the others.

'How are you?'

'I'm rightly.'

'Did they not tell you I was coming?'

'I'm the last one to know anything in here. They tell me nothing.'

He likes to hold me at arm's length.

'I think you've put on some weight.'

'They're making me drink those high-protein strawberry things all the time.'

'You weren't looking after yourself at home. That's why you were down to six stone.'

He takes me for a walk in the walled garden stopping here and there to look at what plants are beginning to bud.

Christopher says, 'You're shivering.'

'It's freezing.'

'No, it's not.'

'It would skin a fairy.'

'I'll have to buy you a winter coat.'

'Don't bother your head. I wouldn't get the wear out of it.'

'I'm only joking.'

'The price of things nowadays would scare a rat.'

Sometimes of late I get a bit dizzy, become a bit of a staggery Bob. I bump into him coming down a step.

'Careful.'

He takes me, not by the elbow, but by the hand.

'Your tiny hand is frozen,' he says and laughs. 'I have a meeting with the doctors now.'

'Is that my window there?'

'No, you're on the other side of the building.'

'Do you ever hear anything of that brother of mine?' Christopher looked at me as if I had two heads.

'Paul's dead.'

'Jesus mercy.' I nearly fell down again, had to hold on hard to Christopher's arm. 'When did this happen?'

'Last year.'

'Why was I not told?'

'You were. He had a severe stroke.'

'Where?'

'At his home. In Belfast. I've told you all this many times.'

'Well it's news to me. Poor Paul. We were always very great. God rest him.' And then my chin began manoeuvring and I couldn't stop myself crying.

'Poor Paul.'

'Don't upset yourself so – every time.'

I keep myself very busy in here. I don't mind helping out. When they ask me to set the tables or make up the bed, I don't complain. If I see anything needing done, I do it. Makes me feel less out of place. The way some of them in here leave the wash-basins! And there are other things about toilets . . . it'd scunner you, some people's filthy habits. I draw the line at heavy work, like hoovering or anything like that, I'm not fit for it now but I don't mind going round and giving my own room a bit of a dust. I was always very particular. Or straightening the flowers. The others watch television all the time. They sleep in front of the television, more like. I don't see one of them doing a hand's turn.

But what really galls me, is I can't make Christopher a bite to eat when he comes. All the way from England. Not even a cup of tea. In my day I could make a Christmas dinner for ten. And a good one, at that. Holy Mother of God. And now I struggle to put on my tights.

Eugene Anthony was baptised not long after he was born – they suspected something, but they never told me. I was kept in the dark as usual. From start to finish. They've done something strange to my ears – that time they removed the rodent ulcer. My ears have never been right since. Black and as hard as the hammers of Newgate. It feels like they've put them on backwards too.

I'm sitting in the recreation room with the rest of them. They're nearly all sleeping. Chins on chests. There's a thing on the wall.

WELCOME TO EDENGROVE
TODAY IS FRIDAY
The date is 1st
The month is March
The year is 2001
The weather is cloudy
The season is winter

Christopher has let me down. Badly. Doesn't believe in God any more. That was the worst slap in the face I've ever had –

as a mother. Said it to me one night in a taxi. Talk about a bolt from the blue. After the education I put him through. What a waste. With his opera and jumping on and off planes and all the rest of it. In one of the most Catholic cities in the world. It's a far cry from the way I was reared – but it doesn't matter what you get up to if you stop practising your religion. If you turn your back on God. What shall it profit a man if he gain the whole world and so shall lose his soul. Never a truer word. But, please God, he'll come round – before it's too late. I pray for him every night. What a terrible waste.

Another terrible slap in the face was the day I had to give-away my niece's baby. In a sweetshop in Newry, of all places. That was where the priest had arranged the meeting. Among the liquorice allsorts and the dolly mixtures. And me having to hand over that wee bundle across the counter. All the more galling for me because of what happened to Eugene Anthony. The family counts at times like that. Everybody weighed in – driving and money and what have you. Of course she should never have had the child in the first place. And her not even considering getting married. I always said that. It was a sin – utterly wicked. So bad the whole thing had to be hushed up. There wasn't one of the neighbours knew a thing about it, thank God. She went to the Good Shepherd nuns for her confinement. Someplace they have on the Border. It's funny that, the way it doesn't show, sometimes – the way they can hide it. If they've done wrong. Something to do with the muscles – holding it in. There might be something else . . .

Maybe the best way to pass is to do nothing. That way

you can't make mistakes. So just sit your ground. Take nothing under your notice. But that way they'll say there's something wrong – she's not in the same world as the rest of us. Doolally, in fact.

I sees a doctor and a nurse – it was wee Gerard without the moustache – come into the recreation room. And of all things! they have Christopher with them. That doctor looks too young. His hair sticks up like a crew cut.

'Christopher – when did you arrive?'

'We'll go to your room – it's quieter – for a chat,' he says.

'My name is on the door.'

I love it when he holds my hand like I'm his girlfriend. In my room we all get settled. And right away I get a bad feeling even though Gerard folds his arms and smiles at me. There's something about the way Christopher is clearing his throat.

'Well, we've come to a decision but we want to involve you in it,' he says. 'You know how you've been losing weight and not looking after yourself. And singeing the curtains with holy candles? You could have burned the house down, and yourself with it.' I just keep shaking my head. 'For six weeks or so the doctors and nurses in here have been building up a picture of you – and it's their opinion that it would be a danger for you to go back to living alone. Even with help and support. Now as you know it's impossible for me to come home and look after you. So the best option for you is residential care.'

'I wasn't born yesterday.'

'What d'you mean?'

138

'That's an old people's home.'

'It's not like that nowadays. Not like the old days . . .'

'The accommodation is state of the art,' says the doctor with the crew cut.

'They have their own hairdressers and chiropodists,' says Gerard. 'Cassie's a great one for the style.'

'Believe me, I've researched this.' This time it's Christopher talking. I'm getting confused about who's saying what. I keep looking from one to the other – watching if their mouth is moving, wondering if my backwards-on ears are playing me up. 'There are people who thrive when they go into such places. They've been alone at home – isolated and lonely – and find it's great to meet new people of their own age.'

'Not if they're all doolally, like in here. Who wants company like that?'

'I'll have a look around at the various options. Choose the best place or, at least, the best place with a vacancy. But we might have to wait a while. Dr Walsh here says every where is full at the moment. And you can't go home. It would be dangerous – you might set up another shrine and burn the place to the ground.'

'I would not.'

'I'm only joking, Mother.' Christopher smiles and puts his hand on mine. 'But it has to be your decision. We are not putting you in. We're telling you what the situation is and letting you decide. The doctors are saying you'd be best in residential care. And I think I agree with that. But the decision is yours.'

'Well, if it's for the best.' I hear the words coming out of me and they are not the words I mean to say. I go on saying things I don't mean. Why am I doing this? Why am I saying this? 'I don't want to be a nuisance. What'll we do if there's no places?'

'Not to worry, Dr Walsh says you can stay on here until we get somewhere.'

'People die,' says Gerard.

'Somewhere nice. Overlooking the sea – out at Bray. Or the North Side, Howth maybe.'

'The North Side – yes.'

It's dark. There's a strip of light under the door. If I turn to the wall I'll not see it. Away in the distance somebody's clacking plates. You can't lock that door. Anybody could come in. And climb into the bed. That oul man rummaging in his pyjama bottoms.

I want to be in my own house. With my own things around me. My china cabinet, my bone-handled knives and forks. The whole set's no longer there. But after so many years, what would you expect – wee Christopher digging with soup spoons. I'm like a penny bap gone stale in the window – I've no say. I don't want to be a nuisance. That's the last thing I want to be. I've no idea how long I've been in here. All I know is that I'd like to go home, if you wouldn't mind. Maybe my brother in Belfast could help. Paul is so methodical. Maybe – even better – if I got Christopher on to them he could sort it out – go and talk to the doctors. Convince them. And I could go home . . .

UP THE COAST

She came into the gallery the next day by herself. The bell chinked as she opened the door. The place was full of sunlight. The boy on the desk looked up. He recognised her and blushed a little. How sweet. He was in shirtsleeves. She asked if he'd gotten away at a reasonable hour the night before. He smiled and said it was OK. There hadn't been too much mess and nobody'd got *very* drunk, which was almost unheard of. And the wine had been a better choice than usual. It had really been a great opening. He had the loveliest eyes. Had she seen any reviews yet? She shook her head. No. She wasn't emotionally robust enough for that at the minute. Especially when her life's work was involved. One thing at a time. He smiled and nodded as if he understood. She was more apprehensive that there was to be a profile in the *Guardian* magazine. With a yet-to-be-taken photo. But she said nothing about this in case he'd think she was showing off.

He congratulated her on her sales. The fourteen works available to buy had all gone. Somehow last night there had been a feeling of stampede. Red stickers kept appearing and some people felt they were going to miss out.

'The hair may be turning grey but I'm not dead yet,' she kept saying to everyone. 'There's more to come.'

Last night had been so fraught with people that she wanted to have another, more contemplative look on her own. She hadn't selected the pictures for the retrospective herself nor had she had anything to do with the hanging. It had all been done by the gallery.

The three white rooms were empty and utterly quiet. In the first, the sunlight fell on the boards of the floor. They creaked a little as she put her weight on them. She took out her glasses to read the labels. Only one or two things had survived from Art College days. And they were beside her grandchild series. So much for the chronological approach.

The second room was entirely devoted to the four large works to have survived from the Inverannich experience. There were others in various parts of the world but to have called them in would have been too expensive. She let her eyes traverse the space. They were good. All four of them. They each had something different to say. The stones took on a life of their own – like Plath's mushrooms. Strong, elbowing forward, butting for attention. Our story must be told. They had *become* the dispossessed, the abused – in contrast to the abject submission of the people of Inverannich as they'd left. The homesickness – the wrench from the land and everything dear to them. She'd read somewhere of the wailing and lamentation – the processions of people with a lifetime's paraphernalia making their way to the boats. It was a subject done by one of her favourite painters, William McTaggart, in the last century. Three times he returned to it – the emigrant ship. It waits in the distance as the departing boat rows towards it. Figures twisted with grief and loss merge with the rocks on the foreshore. In his last canvas, above the waiting ship is a barely perceptible fragment of rainbow.

Her almost abstract rendering of these same events in greys and greens, blacks and yellows brought her back to the anger at their making – the cross-hatching, the savaging of the paper surface. Always she wanted to be open to the accidental. These large works had been done from sketches and notebooks she'd retrieved from her camp the summer after. They were part of the healing process. Of the cat there had been no sign.

Alongside each was a framed picture with compartments. Every item – be it a grey stone or an oystercatcher's feather or a limpet shell or a page of a notebook – had a compartment to itself within the frame. They had the beauty of being themselves as well as the balance they achieved against or alongside one another. The cheap tear-off notebook pages with their pale blue lines covered in her dense, distinctive scribble had yellowed after so many years – changed colour like verdigris on sculpture – as they'd come to an accommodation with their surroundings.

Several works in the third room had been landscapes painted onto assemblies of these same writings and sketches – page after page after page, their content partly obscured by rough brush strokes – sea colours of Prussian blue and ultramarine. She approached one of the works and adjusted her glasses on the bridge of her nose to read the handwriting. Her handwriting. Her thoughts from so long ago made her cringe. Had she been so self-important? It was something about the tone:

Day 2.

I am amazed at the changes in the light here – not hour to hour, but minute to minute. So difficult to pin down. The landscape and seascape has such colour. I'd like to be able to do an Ivon Hitchens here but inhabited – highlighting the transience of people in such a place as this – borders and boundaries between one colour and the next, the shade and light. The balance between representation and allowing the paint its head.

When I get time to sit down and look around me this place is truly amazing. Yesterday was about practicalities. When I landed it was wet and blustery and the mountains, whose shape I knew from the April visit, had disappeared altogether. Shrouded, as they say. The black rocks in the bay spilled with white waterfalls after being swamped by wave after wave. Worst possible conditions for putting up a tent.

Today is what is required. The sky is blue and cloudless, the mountains magnificent. Green foothills become sand dunes, become the beach. Most black rocks are covered with lichen the colour of mustard. And the sea. It is such a presence continually roaring onto the beach. Waves are amazing things. Far out they rise as dark parallels. The best moment is when they break, the dark turquoise colour before the white spills curving down the face. Then the white spreads its length with a roar. On the gravel beaches to the north as the wave rushes in – the crest has such force it sets the tiny black stones hopping against the white foam.

It's always changing. Far out it is grey – it is blue – it is slate – it is shining like the bevel of a blade where it meets the sky. Was anything ever so straight as the line at the horizon?

From the maps the peninsula is about 30 miles long and at its narrowest about 10 miles wide. Where I am – the north-west – it's wild and virtually uninhabited – except for deer. I have a notion that it is only here, in solitude, that I might encounter my true self. With no interruptions I will become more and more conscious of myself and my place, however microscopic, in the universe. But then again I read somewhere about one of the medieval monks who refused to go on pilgrimage. 'If God was overseas, d'you think I'd be here?' Maybe it's the same with art. Maybe I should have stayed at home and worked.

*   *   *

The next morning he got up early and made himself some sandwiches. He buttered slices of white bread and filled them with the only thing in the fridge – cheese. He used his hunting knife to cut away the mildewed faces from the block even though there were plenty of knives in the drawer. He smeared the cheese with tomato ketchup.

The light was clear and harsh. It would be a good day. The sea was the right colour. He washed his blade under the tap, wiped it dry on a towel and returned it to its sheath at his waist. The sandwiches he wrapped in waxed paper from around the loaf. His Dad complained that bread went stale out of its wrapper. Fuck him, he could make toast. Anyway he'd still be too pissed from the night before to notice. Plus a hangover.

He walked down into the village, the sea on his right-hand side. Gulls squawked and screamed. After yesterday's storm there was no wind at all – smoke rose straight up from Loudan's chimney. Just as he passed the bastard came out his back door with a shovel in his hand and waved to him. Nod the head – that's enough for that cunt. The fishing boat must have sailed at first light or when the storm died down. There was a gap where it had tied up the night before. Brown seaweed had blown onto the road and there were strings of it caught up on Loudan's wire fence.

He stopped at the hotel above the harbour and went round the back to see if anybody was up. Plastic crates and aluminium kegs were stacked beneath the kitchen window. Bottle caps of different colours were all over the yard and embedded in the mud at the back door. He arched his hand between the side of his head and the glass and tried to see into the kitchen. Empty stout bottles, a filled ashtray, a mug of tea not drunk from the night before. If he got anybody out of bed they'd tell him to fuck off. He sat down on the rim of an aluminium keg to wait.

After a while he heard a woman coughing. A lavatory flushed and the water rattled down inside the pipe at his shoulder. He stood and waited. Old Jenny came into the kitchen and put the kettle on. He knocked the frosted glass of the kitchen door.

'Who is it?'

'It's me,' he said.

Jenny drew the bolt and opened the door.

'Whatdya want at this time of the morning?'

'I need a couple of cans.'

The door swung open and he stepped inside. Jenny bent to light a cigarette at the blue flame beneath the kettle. She coughed and her face became red and pumped up. She steadied herself with her hand on the draining board until the fit of coughing was over.

'Aw Christ I'm dying.' She lifted the keys and went into the hallway. He followed her.

'Three Super lager.'

Jenny opened the bar. The place smelt of beer and stale cigarette smoke. The curtains were still pulled and it was almost dark. She switched on the light behind the bar and ducked beneath the counter. He watched her through the slats of the drawn shutters. She was still clearing her throat from the coughing.

'That was some night last night,' she said. 'Those ones from the north are wild men.'

'Aye – anyone off the boats is mad. And twenty Regal.' She put the cans in the pocket of her apron and came out bent double from beneath the counter flap. He could have got her like that – with a single rabbit punch. The oul girl was sticking her neck out. She straightened and set the things on the counter among last night's dirty glasses.

'It's a good day,' he said.

'I haven't had time to look yet.'

He tugged each can from its plastic loop and slipped one in each side pocket. The last one he zippered into his breast pocket with the sandwiches. The empty plastic loops he threw on the bar.

'Could you put it on the slate? The boss knows. He says it's OK.'

Jenny looked at him and shook her head.

'I'll tell him.'

You will too, y'oul hoor.

He set out at a good pace. His Ammo boots were very quiet for the size of them. Boots that big should've given more warning. After a couple of hours the road began to show a line of grass and weeds in the middle. He passed the last house, burned and left derelict some twenty years ago, and the road reduced to a track. The sun was becoming hotter and the effort of walking fast made him feel sweaty. His Dad would be up now – snarling and eating his toast. In the hotel Jenny would be adding water to the packets of 'home-made broth'. The track veered off to the sea. Sometimes farmers took a tractor-load of gravel off the beach but nothing had been up here for months.

He left the track and headed up the hill. His boots rattled through the heather and the sky was full of the sound of

larks. He looked up but could see nothing. The hill was steep
at this point and he had to lean into it stepping up like stairs
– pressing on his thighs with his hands. Every now and then
he would stop to get his breath back, breathing through his
mouth. He should really give up the fags. There was a good
view from here but it would be better from the top. When
the noise of his breathing disappeared he heard a grasshopper.
And insects came in, buzzing close to his ear, then away again.
You never know. You never know what might happen. It was
just luck there had been a storm and the fishing boat had
been driven in to shelter. The crew had been good crack. He
didn't remember everything they'd said – there had been too
much drink taken – but he remembered enough. The boys
off the boats had always plenty of money and bought drink
like there was no tomorrow. You could be on the edge of
company like that and get pished without them knowing you
couldn't afford your round. He was always broke. But what
else could he be? He was for the most part unemployed.
Sometimes he did a bit of gardening – grass cutting and tidying
up for cash. Occasionally, on account of his father, he'd get
a day or two's work on a clam boat but he was prone to
throwing up and began making excuses when he was asked.
He tried the Army but it coincided with an appearance at
the Sheriff Court for having a go at a cunt of a bus driver –
he'd had a few drinks and the driver kept yapping on about
not smoking, even though there was hardly anybody on the
fucking bus. So he gubbed him. After that the Army didn't
want to know – the bastards. So cash was a novelty.

It was the fishing-boat skipper who had told them about her. It was him who'd dropped her off a couple of weeks ago. Up here on the mountain – now – he was getting a hard-on just thinking about it. He put his hands down the front of his trousers and arranged it so that he was more comfortable. Not yet. He was only looking – sniffing around.

Day 6.

Hadn't time to write anything yesterday. But there will be days like that. I am not going to oblige myself like some kind of schoolgirl to annotate each day. What is important is that I make things based on the nature of these ruins. That's the priority. Whether paintings or sculptures or photographs or notes towards such things. And yet the diary keeping is important to give a perspective of the overall project.

The more I try to render these networks of tumbled walls – the danger is to make them not abstract enough – the more I feel the presence of the people who lived here a hundred and fifty years ago. They were me and the likes of me before they were driven out by hunger and landlords.

I am outside in my sleeping bag because of the cold, sitting with my back to a stone wall writing this. The fire is cracking and hissing. The gathering of driftwood is one of my favourite chores. I walk the foreshore and spy dead branches and planks and whoop and pounce on them and drag them back. My Uncle would have been proud of me. It was him told me about this place. When he was stationed at the airfield during the war he came here many times. According to him in the mid-1800s the people of the village were evicted by the landlord, Lord Somebody-or-other, to make way for sheep. Or maybe they'd fled of their own accord in search of a better life, away from constant famine, leaving their homes to tumble. He said it was full of ghosts. Inverannich, he called it. 'A deserted village but you'll not find it on any map.' The ruins provide some shelter for my tent. The sea must have encroached since this place was built because it seems too close, too threatening. I can hear it now. On my doorstep, if a tent can be said to have a doorstep.

Day 8.

Hot, idyllic weather. Blue sky and calm water. Tiny wavelets wash in – a kind of tongue roll – just one at a time. The sea is mirror flat reflecting the sky. Black and yellow bladderwrack breaks the surface between the dark rocks which are covered with tiny white pin limpets.

Pools gather where they can on the black rocks and are edged with lettuce-green seaweeds. 'You would never want a nicer day than this.' I say it out loud to myself and the sound of my voice startles me. I realise I have not spoken for a week and have almost forgotten how to do so. I resolve to practise. At night, it being utterly clear, I look up at the stars transfixed. I say aloud, 'You would never want a nicer night than this.' My voice is strained because my head is back looking up. Pressure on the rusty vocal cords.

I just adore the solitude this week so far. Not a man-made sound, no smell of exhausts or cigarettes, not an artefact, except that which is washed up – the odd light bulb, plastic syringes, condoms, some trays each with an indentation to rest your glass. One of which I rescued for my own use. When you do lift your head here, whether it's rain or shine, you see something worth looking at. Watching TV is a way of not thinking. Being by yourself in this remote place forces you into certain modes of thought and action. Work, apart from the main purpose, is a way of entertaining yourself. Making paintings passes the time. Indeed I know of nothing better for that purpose. If you start to make a painting after breakfast the next time you look up it will be supper time. All the time you have been thinking, making decisions – this or that? Darker or lighter? Is this line good enough? How to incorporate the ghosts without actually showing them?

I now know the surprise Robinson Crusoe must have felt when he came across the footprint.

A little further on he came across a stream, rising up. If you looked closely you could see pale flecks of sand rising and falling with the force of the spring. There was nothing purer than that. The source of a mountain stream.

Out of the corner of his eye he saw a herd of red deer. Property of the fuckin gentry. They don't like you moving about on the hills – warn you off. Not personally – but there's notices all over the place. On gates, on fences. You're liable to be accidentally shot, they say. There's more chance of being hit by a fuckin meteor. What they really don't want is the dregs parading about their hills. Especially when they've spent hours stalking beasts and suddenly some cunt like me walks over the hill and they're off. Fuckin zoom, never to be seen again.

He took out his binoculars and focused. The stag was out on his own, away from the hinds. It had a good spread of antlers and just as he watched it, it put its head back and barked. If he had a gun – the right kind of rifle with a scope – he could bring it down from here. No bother. A seven-millimetre Mauser snug between his cheek and his shoulder. The bastard would run for a hit, then crumple. Just like a chicken with its head chopped off. Or it would fall just where it stood – all legs and awkwardness, collapsing like an ironing board.

He had read in a magazine how to butcher a deer but had never had the chance to do it in practice. Rabbits he could skin, no bother – like pulling off a jumper.

The saw-toothed Bowie had arrived by post from the catalogue and he was surprised that it came up to his expectations. In fact it was bigger than he thought it would be. The blade was made of superb carbon steel which produced such a sweet ping when he plucked it with his fingernail.

He got up from his sitting position and broke the skyline. The herd galloped away. He climbed now with the determination that he would reach the top in one. Establish a rhythm. Pace the breathing. There was a pain barrier but once through that everything settled down. Sweat ran down his face and dripped from his chin. His thighs hurt but he continued stepping up. Over the top and then that view – headlands, islands and the Atlantic Ocean. Next stop America. He ran hop jumping down the other side. When he came to another stream he flopped down and immersed his face, then drank. The water was cold enough to make his teeth hurt.

Beside the spring was a kind of cliff face. He got his back against it. He smoked a cigarette and stared down at his tan boots. Here he could defend himself no matter what came at him. He liked the feeling he had in caves – with his back protected. That way there was no situation he couldn't cope with. He could light a fire, kill a rabbit, catch a fish, he could survive. He read in the papers of these people who died of exposure on mountains, hill walkers even. Accountants from Manchester, fuckin hippies from Leeds. It would never happen to him because he knew how to handle himself.

He put all three cans into the water twisting and embedding them into the gravel. The sun was hot for June. He stripped to the waist and spread his T-shirt on the rock to let the sweat dry. His tattoo caught his eye and he liked it all over again. The one word. Simple. The granite held the heat of the sun and was comfortably warm as he leaned his back against it. He had been on the move for about four hours now and was starving.

*

154

He took his knife from its sheath, unwrapped his sandwiches and cut them in two. He sat looking down at the coastline. There was no sign of her. But then he hardly expected to see her first thing. There would have to be a bit of stalking. He chewed each bite ten times to get the best out of it. The long waves rolled in as far as he could see.

He couldn't wait for the can to really cool down. He reached over and unstuck one and jerked the ring-pull. The lager exploded all over his face and chest.

'Aw fuck.' He laughed and held the frothing hole to his mouth. He drank until the lager was under control. A bite of the sandwich, a swill of the lager. The sun. This was it. Nobody to get on his wick. Just himself. When the can was finished he wondered if he should have another. Better not. They might come in useful. A can each.

When he had finished eating there was some cheese and tomato on the blade of his knife. He licked the food off then stabbed the blade into the sandy earth to clean it. It made the sound of the word sheath each time he drove it in. Sheath – sheath – sheath. He scanned the west side with his binoculars but could see nothing. He smoked a cigarette. Sometimes he thought the only reason he ate food was for the pleasure of having a cigarette afterwards.

Last night he'd been sitting – by himself as usual – on a stool at the far end of the bar when the skipper and his crew came in and told the story – said she had just arrived at the pier with a rucksack the size of herself and offered money to be dropped off by the deserted village at Inverannich.

'Was she . . . ?' The barman raised an eyebrow.

'She made you pay attention – if that's what you mean.'

'She was a cracker,' said the youngest fisherman – and growled softly into his beer.

There was a slight breeze at this height which cooled him. He stood and unzipped his fly and pissed on the rocks and surrounding heather – like an animal marking its territory.

He did not want to pollute the spring. He retrieved his cans from the water and zippered them into the pocket of his anorak along with the T-shirt and the binoculars. He tied its arms around his waist and moved on, bare-backed, his hands free.

The journey down was so much faster. Parts of the hill were covered in scree and he ran down these in great leaping steps. The stones clicked hollow for the brief second his boots were in contact. Lower down the scree changed to peat and heather and tussocky grass. It was like dancing – the feet had to be just right – at the right angle – doing the right steps for the terrain. This way and that. A dog's hind leg. His eyes to the ground, watching for trouble. A zigzag.

He was in good shape – proud of himself. Lean and muscled. Like an athlete without ever having trained. But he was too white. His tan of last summer had gone. When he reached the bottom his instinct was to run and wipe the sweat from his face in the sea but he stopped. He would leave footprints the whole way across the sand. He wasn't ready to declare himself yet. So far it was only a bit of noseying – see what he could see, kind of thing. Nothing set in stone. Opportunity knocks. Whatever will be, will be. Kiss her ass, her ass.

This was easy walking – light, short grass growing out of sandy soil. He headed north keeping off the beach. The ground sprung beneath his feet. There were flowers all over the place. Blue ones, pink ones.

In the pub the youngest guy had said he thought she was game.

'She'd give you two dunts for every one of yours.'

The skipper wasn't so sure.

'That's the wee boy in you talking.' He put on a baby voice and said, 'The size of dick I want is a *big* dick.'

'Fuck off.'

They all laughed and ordered more drinks. He didn't know what was said next because he announced he was going for a crap. The barman winked and said, 'You're so full of shit it's coming out your arse.'

'Any more of that and I'll take my slate somewhere else.'

When he came back from the toilet the skipper was still talking about the girl.

'Naw,' he said, 'they'll be as happy as Larry on their own up there.'

'They?' said the barman.

'She took one of the cats with her – just as we were getting ready to go. One of the ones that hang about the pier. Anyway she grabbed a big kitten – for company, she says.'

'I told you,' said the youngest guy. 'She's lonely – up there all by herself.'

'He nearly missed the boat,' the skipper waved his thumb at the boy, 'running to get her cat food. To get in with her.'

Day 10.

Swimming in my swimming pool is a real treat. It's only about twenty yards away. There are a series of flat rocks jutting into the sea like a natural pier. The first one is like a slightly tilted raft which is great for sunbathing. At high tide the rock rises a couple of feet above the sea. The water is turquoise green because of its depth and the immaculate sandy bottom. I've seen grey fish moving down below – mullet maybe. It is also sheltered because the next outcrop of rock shields it from the open sea. The whole thing is a wonderful rectangular-shaped gully. If I was a geography teacher I'd take a photo as an example of a fault – you can see the strata. I might even put it on the classroom wall labelled – 'My fault'. You can dive straight in – it's like a diving board. I can't touch the bottom, even when I do. It's a freedom like no other – swimming in your pelt. I feel like an otter, a seal. The water cradles me, soothes me, caresses me, cleanses me. You feel clothed in it except for the fact that it's freezing. The first plunge is the worst. But that's the way it has got to be done – no testing the waters here – it gets all the pain over in an instant. If the midges get really annoying this is the best refuge.

He climbed the next headland and when he reached the top lay down. Beneath him the sandy bay was full of black rocks with cliffs at the back. His stomach tightened. There were footprints all over the place. Someone hadn't bothered to hide the fact that they were there. He scanned the beach with his binoculars but could see no sign of movement. There was a river cutting across the sand and emptying into the sea. Further inland he saw a network of grey tumbled walls where houses had been. Suddenly in the lenses a flash of blue. He backtracked. A blue tent. Her place. A half-hour passed and still there was no sign of movement. He would venture down.

He walked on the flat table rocks. They were fissured and creased like old skin. He had to go the long way, leaping from rock to rock, so as not to leave his prints. When he reached an area where the sand had been churned up he left the rocks and moved as quietly as he could across the sand. Near the tent was a dead fire among some slabs. On a rock were three pairs of women's pants which had dried in the sun. They were the same shape. Two white and a black. Each was pinned down with a fist-sized stone.

The tent was pitched in the shelter of two old stone walls. Further back against another tumbled wall was a wind-break of the same blue material. There appeared to be no one about. He moved the flap of the tent which had been left open. He put his head inside. It was damp and smelt faintly of plastic and fungus.

There was a red rucksack with a sleeping bag rolled on top of it. A pot, a kettle, a large Winsor & Newton sketch-book, some tins of Heinz beans, some packets of dried cat food, a small Primus stove with blue canisters of gas. A used tin held paintbrushes and pencils beside packs of

Polaroid film. He stepped outside and looked all around. No sign of anyone. Inside again he went to the rucksack. The zipper was already undone and he just flipped the top open. There was a black purse, which he opened. A handful of coins, bank cards wedged into their sections, a library card. In the wallet part there were three ten-pound notes which he folded and slipped into his pocket. He put the purse back where he found it – on top of a mauve jumper – and unzipped one of the side pockets. A box of tampons. Other pockets contained – a face-cloth, a book called *The Letters of Vincent Van Gogh*, a washbag with a toothbrush and stuff in it. The only thing of any interest was a half-bottle of brandy with very little out of it.

There was a hardback notebook. He spun through the pages with his thumb. It was blank except for the beginning pages. Here her writing was very neat and in straight lines even though there were no lines to guide the writing. The white paper took on a faint blueness from the tent:

Day 12.

I can hardly believe that three weeks ago I was in Art College. How awful that place was – spreading the new barbarism. They substitute randomness for creativity. They use the camera and the video now instead of brush and charcoal. The more clumsy and amateurish the result the better it's liked. Pass the responsibility for art onto the viewer (I know I have a Polaroid but it's useful for documenting work – they can even be works themselves).

*Mum and Dad were both painters so when I went to
Art College I expected something better . . .*

His eye trailed away from the words and he closed the
book. He lifted the sketchbook and looked at the first page.
It was fucking awful. So was the painting on the next page.
And the next. Like somebody was cleaning different colours
off their brush. Greens, purples, browns. If her mother and
father were painters she was fucking adopted. Black scribbles
were like what he'd done in school trying to wear down the
lead of his pencil.

He set the sketchbook down where he found it and ducked
outside the tent. The only thing stored in the wind-break
was firewood, dry driftwood. He went back to the tent and
unzipped the pocket of his anorak at his waist. He set a can
of Super lager on an oval rock. She could take that two ways
- either as a gift or else it would scare the shit out of her.

And he was away jumping from the churned-up sand at
the camp-site to the flat rocks and then up the hill to a
position where he could watch for her coming back. It was
late afternoon and there was a drop in temperature with
the breeze coming off the sea. He spread his anorak on the
grass and lay down. With his elbows resting on the ground
the binoculars were steady and he could see much more
through them. He kept his T-shirt off to get tanned by the
breeze but after an hour or so he began to feel cold and
put it on again. Various trails of her footsteps led nowhere
in particular. He looked again at the knickers drying on the

rock. He began to get a hard-on thinking about her. If he pulled himself off now it might spoil things. He had held off for so long he might as well wait a bit longer.

He imagined her walking up the hill behind him and surprising him when he was doing it. Might be good that – turn her on, maybe. He was hungry and tried to think about food to distract himself. New potatoes and butter. A fish supper. Wagon Wheels. Chocolate was good for energy in survival situations.

A pair of oystercatchers were creating a racket further up the beach – peep – peep – peep – peep. They were swooping and diving, going mad because somebody was approaching their nest. Something bad was going to happen. Was this her coming? He focused his binoculars on the birds, then on the landscape beneath where they were creating the fuss. Maybe it was a stoat or something like that. He saw movement and tried to keep the binoculars as still as possible. It was a black cat. Strolling out of the sand dunes. It was followed by a boy – walking – carrying a board or something. What the fuck was *he* doing here? Nobody mentioned *him*. He banged the binoculars down onto the grass. Keep watching – the girl is probably with him. In the vicinity. He looked again at the boy. About a mile away he looked young, around fifteen or so – walking barefoot carrying this board in one hand and his sandals in the other.

He tried to remember the conversation in the pub. He had been overhearing it – not taking part in it. Maybe he'd missed something important – one of the times he'd gone to the gents. Or had they said something he forgot because too much drink had been taken? Without the binoculars he watched the tiny figure and the cat approaching. The cat did not walk to heel like a dog but ran this way and that, towards the sea, into the dunes. It sat and got left behind, then caught up. The boy paid no attention to it. He approached the tent and set his board on a rock. Through the binoculars he could see the boy was wearing khaki shorts – bare-chested, his shirtsleeves knotted around his neck, his shirt protecting his back from the sun. He disappeared into the tent.

Almost immediately he came out again. He now had his shirt on. Then he spotted the can of Super lager. He looked all around, scanned the bay and the hills. He looked towards where he lay with his binoculars. The boy must have had good eyesight because he spotted him immediately and waved. Fuck it. Maybe the binoculars had flashed – maybe his stupid head had been sticking up. He felt he had to wave back.

He got up and slung his anorak over his shoulder and decided to go down. When he got there the boy was sitting on a rock sipping the can.

'Hi – was this meant for me?'

It was a girl. Jesus. Her red hair was cropped very close. He had been looking at her tits through the binoculars and hadn't even noticed – hadn't even paid attention to them. She'd been walking half naked.

'Hi,' he said.

'It was very thoughtful of you. Cheers.' She saluted him with the can. English, by the sound it. He pulled out the other can and jerked off the ring-pull. It exploded but this time he had the can aimed away from himself.

'*Sláinte*.' He returned her salute.

'Oh yes – slanchay.' She smiled and tilted the can up to her mouth. He had a small tattoo on his forearm of the word *Mother*. The heart was red, the rest of the design, navy.

'So what brings you all this way?' he said.

She laughed, 'I'm an *artiste*.' She made fun of the word. 'Trying to be creative. And what brings *you* here? To the world's end?'

'I live here.' He nodded to the south-east. 'Over by.'

'What do you do?'

'As little as possible.' Seeing her look concerned he said, 'Naw – I'm on and off the boats – but it's not regular.'

She was in her early or mid-twenties. It was hard to tell exactly.

'That's miles away. I meant what brings you to this place.' She gestured all around her.

'They said there was an old village.'

'Yeah.'

'And that there was somebody here.'

'Where did you hear that?'

'In the pub. The guys in the fishing boat from the north.'

'Oh, did they come back?'

He nodded. 'They sheltered for a bit last night. Did you get that storm?'

'Yeah, for sure. Horrendous. My tent nearly took off.' She laughed. 'They were lovely – especially the skipper. They

couldn't do enough for me. So friendly. And you came all
this way . . . ?'

'Yeah.' He stared at her.

'How sweet of you.' He looked away. She called the cat,
'Psh-wsh-wsh,' rubbing her fingers together. But the cat hung
back.

'It's wary of you,' she said. 'Wary of strangers.'

'It's you that's the stranger.' She looked hard at him for
a moment then smiled. He said, 'What's your excuse?'

'For being here?'

He nodded.

'Oh – a lot of reasons,' she said. 'I wanted to be on my
own for a bit. Completely. And . . . I've just finished College.
Art College. And . . . I wanted to do some work. And . . .'
She looked all around her as if she couldn't believe what she
was seeing. 'And to be in this place. It's the most beautiful
place I have *ever* been.'

'Eh?'

'Yes – I never knew there was so much sky. If you live
in a city you just never see it. And the stars at night. But
I'm not here to do just landscapes,' she put inverted commas
in the air with her fingers, 'but to register my *feeling* for
landscape.' She smiled at him. He looked up at the sky. It
was beginning to cloud over from the west. 'It's so remote.
A great-uncle of mine was stationed up here with the RAF
during the war – and he never stopped talking about it. He
said this whole area was the most underpopulated land mass
in the whole of Britain.'

'Because everyone living here's a bastard.' At first she smiled at this. He sat on a rock of his own. He took a long swill from his can of beer. 'English?'

'Born in England.' She laughed and shrugged her shoulders. 'Brought up in Edinburgh. You?'

'Here.'

'What's your name?' She waited for an answer but he just looked over his shoulder out to sea. Then he finished his beer and bent the can in the middle and set it on the rock.

'That was quick.' She was still sipping hers, barely tilting it. She pulled her knees up to her chin and encircled her legs with her arms.

'Do you have moles?' He was looking at her legs.

'No.' She laughed at the directness of his question.

'What's those?' He pointed. She looked down at the underside of her thigh and reached out a finger to touch the black thing on her skin.

'Not again.'

'Ticks,' he said.

'Nearly every day now.'

'There's another one.'

He pointed to the back of her ankle.

'I hate them.'

'You're their dinner. Any nail-polish remover?'

'Forty miles from nowhere? Does that kill them?'

'It gets them off your skin.'

'I just pull them off.'

'I bet they like that.'

'What do you mean?' She looked hard at him, not sure of what he'd said. Whether he meant it or not.

'Never mind. Doing that leaves the head in you. Then you get diseases and everything. They'll scar you for life if you do that. Want me to get them off so's they'll not leave a mark?'

She seemed unsure, but nodded. He pulled out his knife and watched her face.

'Relax,' he said. She became flustered and straightened her legs so that her feet touched the sand.

'It doesn't matter,' she said. 'They're no big deal.'

He came and knelt in front of her.

'Stand up then.' She balanced her can of beer on the rock beside her and slowly got to her feet. He was still kneeling.

'Turn around. Put your hands on your knees.' She did as he told her. He took a cheap plastic lighter from his trouser pocket. His hand was shaking badly. He tried to get it to light. She was conscious of him looking up her legs.

'I feel ridiculous,' she said and straightened up. 'What are you going to do?'

'Coax them out. Burn their arses off. Wait,' he said. 'Don't move.' He got the lighter to spark and turned the flame down. He held the jet close to the black bulb of the tick's body trying not to burn the skin of her thigh.

'Aaaah.' It was a cry of the fear of being burned more than anything else as she felt the heat. The tick moved and he pulled it away from her skin with his fingers. The touch was brief. Her hand came round her thigh to touch the place. There was a trace of blood on her fingers.

'They crawl up the grass and wait for something to pass – a deer – you – then they jump and hang on. Like grim death.'

'But in a place like this they could wait for ever.'

'Yeah – some of them can survive for years. Anything up to four years, they say.'

'You're a bit of an expert.'

'That cat is probably covered in them.' It was grooming itself on a wall near the tent.

His voice had a shake in it. She could see his knees shivering as he squatted behind her looking up. He held the lighter flame to the other tick behind her ankle. When it was out he rubbed the place. Her skin was hot.

'Is that it?' she asked. There was a long pause.

'I like the view from down here.'

She whirled round and stared at him.

'Did you say what I think you said?'

'Yeah.'

'Why don't you go for a swim and cool off?' She turned and walked quickly towards the tent, her limbs stiff and straight.

'Just kidding,' he called after her. The cat ran to her but she brushed it aside with her foot.

He pocketed the lighter and followed her. She was tidying up. She dropped his buckled beer can into a plastic bag. Then set the rest of her beer on the rock in front of him.

'Ta,' he said, swigging from it. 'I thought Art students

were more broad-minded than that. Nudes and that kinda thing. Always in and out each other's beds.'

She didn't answer. The cat came to where she stood and began to criss-cross in front of her, rubbing its back to and fro against her legs.

'Anyway – nobody up here can swim. Nobody teaches it. The boys on the boats say if your boat goes down, it's better that way.'

She was busying herself doing nothing – lifting things, putting them in the plastic bag – moving items within her living space.

'I would like you to leave,' she said.

'I fuckin live here – you don't.'

She walked past him out of the tent and lifted her washing. Each rock, when she threw it away, bumped heavily on the sand. She rolled the pants up and stuffed them into a side pocket of the rucksack. Without looking at him she said, 'I thought I told you to piss off.'

'Huh!' He mocked her. 'Ladies don't use words like that.'

She refused to answer him again. Eventually he shrugged his shoulders in an exaggerated fashion and wandered off.

He found himself a seat in the sunlight on an outcrop above the beach facing her camp and sat watching her. She ignored him and, sitting outside the tent mouth, attempted to boil a small pot on the Primus. He took out his knife and began stabbing it into the mixture of sand and grass he was sitting on. Again the noise – sheath, sheath – as the blade sank in.

'Fuckin snobby ginger bitch,' he said. The bright flick of

a reflection on one of the stone walls reminded him of something. He angled the blade to catch the sun and directed the beam into the open flap of her tent. A circle lit up the darkness of the back wall. As a child he'd done this with a mirror directing the sunlight into bedrooms along the main street – a disc flicking across flowery wallpaper – intruding into rooms – any room he wanted. What was odd was, even though the mirror was square, the light was always a circle. A woman might be taking off her clothes and see a bright spot on the wall and think nothing of it. But it was important to him, down on the street, directing the power of the light. Now he aimed the reflection into her space and the image was still round even though it came from a long narrow blade. He realised what he was seeing was an image of the sun. He had the power to aim the sun, to aim it into her tent – to flick it over the walls, at the girl's face, down between her legs – anywhere he liked. She became aware of the flash when it struck her face and she tried to wave it away like an irritating insect. He kept it trained on her. She looked at where it was coming from and pointedly turned her back on him to eat from her dish. The next thing she knew he was behind her.

'You really fuckin think you are something, don't you?'

She stood facing away from him. He turned her with a pull of her shoulder. The knife was in his hand, its point upwards.

Her voice had dried in her throat and no words would come out. She felt her legs turn to water.

*

Sometimes she ran, sometimes she walked. Always looking over her shoulder. Not believing. Checking. When she ran she clenched her fists. How awful. How utterly awful. The walking was mostly climbing the hills and the running was mostly on the down slopes, digging her trainers in so as not to go too fast and fall head over heels. To break a bone, to twist an ankle out here would be a disaster. She would probably die. Slowing herself down by planting her feet sideways against her own headlong downward rush. Sometimes to the left, sometimes to the right. Her arms out to the side, her hands splayed for a fall. This way and that – like herringbone – to slow her descent. What a nightmare. She had not slept but had kept the fire going all night. She'd sat or squatted, staring into its glowing heart, trying not to see the pictures it showed her. Her project destroyed. Her life wrecked. To have set out in the dark would have been too dangerous so she waited for first light. And when she rested from her running she cried. Her stomach was contorted, rigid and rippling with nerves. Full of gut knots. Stomach clenching. She had diarrhoea in the long grass. Afraid to look in case there was blood. It came, and she couldn't stop it coming. From nerves. Like the crying. She couldn't help herself. Too far from home to hold on. She remembered as a child wanting to cry – falling, or hearing something hurtful said to her – keeping it all in, holding her face straight until she got into her own room. Then letting it go. Always she kept going south, keeping the sea on her right-hand side. Sometimes it rained, sometimes the sun shone. And the whole time she tried not to think. Or to think local. Immediate. This is a hill. This is a descent. To think practical. Effort needs to be put into this particular climb. Agility needs to be the priority on these rocks. If I come across a sheep path it will get me to some sort of a track which will eventually get me to the tar road. Then a simple walk to the town. Oh fuck. She was so angry. She had never been as angry as this in the whole of her life. Had never used the word fuck, even into herself.

She didn't know how long it took her – most of the day – but eventually she came to the brow of a hill and saw in the far distance a smudge of smoke from the town. It was still a couple of hours away.

It was good to feel tarmac under her feet. On the road into town she saw a doctor's house. Set back off the road behind well-trimmed lawns. There was a brass plate on the railings. She read the surgery times and hesitated. Then walked on into the town. Down by the harbour she was aware that her knees were trembling. She didn't particularly want it, but she knew she needed some food. Her blood sugar must be low. The clock in the grocery shop said 6.30. The Sunday papers were just arriving. At six thirty in the evening? When she opened her purse she saw that the guy had robbed her. With what change he'd left her she bought a sandwich and an orange juice.

'The bastard.' She found a place with her back to the pier where she sat eating and drinking in the sunlight. She was amazed at how utterly changed she was and how it didn't show. In the shop she'd made sentences and spoken and asked for what she wanted. The elderly woman had listened to her and taken her money and smiled a little at the transaction. While she waited for her change she had turned her foot this way and that as if to admire her trainers and bit her fingernails and touched her ear lobe (as she had a habit of doing) and none of what had happened to her the previous day was apparent. Something had profoundly changed and she had no way of showing it. She had no way of talking about it. The outside and the inside. They were not connected. And never would be again.

She needed a plan, needed to take charge of herself. All her drive so far had been focused on returning to the place she started from. That had been simple. Move south. Keep the sea on her right. But now she had to make up her mind what to do.

The doctor's wife cleared the plates from the table to the stainless-steel draining board. When it was just the two of them they ate in the kitchen. Her husband took what red wine remained in his glass to the other room to read the Sunday papers which had just arrived. The doorbell rang and his wife went to answer it. It was a girl.

'Yes?'

'Can I see a doctor?'

'It's Sunday evening. Can't it wait till tomorrow morning?'

'I'm sorry.' The girl was hesitant. 'I didn't know what day it was.'

The doctor's wife smiled and began closing the door.

'Tomorrow morning – ten thirty,' she said. The girl shook her head in some distress.

'I need to see a doctor. I think it's an emergency.'

'What's wrong?' The girl was on the verge of tears and her hands were trembling. 'Are you on holiday?' The girl nodded that she was. 'Just a minute.' When the woman came back to the door she swung it open and ushered the girl in. Then asked her to take a seat in the surgery and left her on her own.

She tried not to think of anything. There was a desk against the wall. The chair she sat in was sideways on to it. On the desk, a blotting pad with leather corners. The room was silent. There were two framed prints on the walls – one of Matisse's abstract coloured-paper cut-out, *The Snail*, the other, Dürer's drawing of a hare. Made in 1502. The place was lit by a frosted glass window, the upper pane was normal. Blue sky, yellow clouds. She liked the way Dürer signed his initials, the way the legs of the A straddled the D. She could hear seagulls. In a distant part of the house, the click of plates and the rattle of a spoon on stainless steel. Against the other wall was a black examination couch covered with a fresh paper towel or sheet. The backs of her thighs were beginning to adhere to the leatherette material of the chair. They made a sound as she moved her weight. She stood when the doctor came in. He indicated that she should sit again, then lowered himself into the swivel chair at the desk.

'What can I do for you?' He was an overweight man in his forties with bushy hair beginning to go grey. His hands were podgy. She looked at his eyes – he had nice dark eyes – then down at her bare knees.

'I'm not sure.' She seemed not to know where to start. 'Just recently I graduated from Art School.'

'In?'

'Drawing and Painting.'

'Where?'

'Edinburgh.'

'My home town. How did you do?'

'Well. At least, I think so,' she said, then added with some hesitation, 'they gave me the Manser Prize as well as a qualification.'

'Congratulations.'

'But that is not what's important,' she said. He smiled, still waiting for her to come to the point. She shook her head – no. 'I wanted to get away from everything. To work. And I got a fishing boat to drop me off at the abandoned village up the coast at Inverannich.'

He nodded waiting.

'I have – I was – several times I was bitten by ticks and I wondered . . . some people say you can become very ill . . .'

He stared at her then stood up from his chair. The lids of his eyes were heavy.

'My wife said you led her to believe this was an emergency.'

'I'm sorry,' she began to cry, 'but I think it is.' The doctor extended his arm indicating the way to the front door.

'If you come back in the morning I'll see you.' Still the girl sat. She was quietly crying making small wet sounds.

'I've been raped,' she said. 'This guy raped me. But I don't want to go to the police.' The doctor was still standing over her. He touched her lightly on the shoulder and it made her crying all the louder. He gave a sympathetic sigh and sat down again. 'He had a knife – a kind of dagger thing . . .'

'Are you injured?'

'I don't know . . . I'm sore.'

'I'm very sorry,' he half shrugged, spread his hands. 'In your own time . . .' She heard him pluck several tissues from a box and they appeared beneath her downturned face. When her crying stopped she dried her face and said, 'I don't want a child out of him. Or a disease. So I came here.'

'I can help with both. Let me get some details first.' He put on a pair of half-moon spectacles and wrote down her particulars. Then he stood and took down a book and opened it flat on his desk. He studied it silently then said as he read, 'We have two daughters of our own, older than you no doubt. Both of them up and away. Can you undress and lie here?' He indicated the examination table. He reached into a cupboard and produced a paper hospital gown which he gave her. 'You may get dressed in this wonderful outfit temporarily.' He pointed to a grey canvas screen.

'Everything?'

'I think it's best.' Then he went out into the hallway and called his wife. There were lowered voices from outside the door.

Behind the screen she undressed, not daring to look into the clothes she took off, embarrassed and scared of what she might see. She put on the nightdress thing – shivering now, yet her armpits were wet with perspiration. She lay on the examination couch and felt it cold even through the paper sheet. The doctor came back into the surgery. He washed and dried his hands, put on latex gloves. The doctor's wife came after him with the colour supplement from the *Observer*.

'Would you like me to hold your hand?' she said.

'No, thanks. I feel not too bad.' The doctor's wife smiled and went to sit by the frosted window, her back to the room. The sound of her turning the pages made the silence of the room even more apparent. The doctor worked quickly – examining, taking samples, giving his patient commands and requests, asking her terrible questions, writing the answers on a pad on his desk. He gave her an injection in her hip which remained in her like a nugget of lead. Occasionally he went back to the desk and consulted his tome – as if it was a recipe book. He looked closely through his glasses at the bruising on her arms which she hadn't noticed before – then over his glasses at her face and the scraped bruise on her forehead. He warned her before he did things like when he used forceps to pluck a few hairs from her head and some from her pubes. He asked her about allergies, then gave her some tablets.

'What are they?'

'Antibiotics. I'll prescribe the rest for you. It's most important you finish the whole course.' He handed her a small plastic tumbler full of straw-coloured water. 'Sorry about the state of the water but it is perfectly safe – it's just peat colouration.' She put the tablets in her mouth and swallowed them down.

'You've picked up another tick on the way here, I see.' With the forceps he slowly drew the creature out of a skin fold at her stomach and pressed a pinch of cotton wool to the pinpoint wound. 'That's the best way to remove them. You shouldn't burn them or put Vaseline on them. Just gently pull them off and treat the wound.' He wiped the black spot onto a tissue and put the forceps in a jar of disinfectant. He gave a sigh and looked up at her. He tapped his temple.

'We can perform effective damage limitation but the real hurt is in here. Very hard to get rid of. They say it keeps coming back. You have to work on the flashbacks. Where are you from?'

'Edinburgh.'

'Yes, yes of course – you said. I'll give you some helpful addresses to contact when you go home.' He touched his wife's shoulder. 'Thank you, love,' and she left the room. On the way out she touched the back of the girl's hand where it lay – gently with her own – almost covering it. Her touch was light and dry and motherly. The girl swung herself off the examination table and sat on the chair again, smoothing the strange textured paper garment beneath her.

'I think the best thing to do,' said the doctor, 'is to proceed as if the law *was* involved. That way you can change your mind later.'

'I won't.'

'Have you washed since . . . ?'

'I've been in the sea.'

'Is that not washing?'

'It's swimming.'

'Do you have a change of clothes?' She shook her head – no.

'Not with me. I just ran first thing this morning.'

'These are what you were wearing at the time?' He looked over at the pile of clothes she had left on the table by the screen. She nodded – yes. 'I'd like to hold onto them. Would you have any objections to wearing some of my daughters' things?'

'I won't change my mind about the police.'

'Fair enough.' He looked her up and down. 'You and my youngest are of a size. She's in Australia.' He excused himself and left the room. He seemed to be away for a long time. She could hear someone treading the floorboards upstairs because they creaked. The ceiling light was a double fluorescent tube.

The doctor came back and put the girl's clothes into a brown paper bag.

'My wife will look after you just now.'

'Thank you.'

'Have you money?' She looked up at him startled. 'Sorry, I mean would you like me to order you a bed and breakfast for tonight?'

'Is there a bank I can go to in the morning?'

'Yes – several.'

She smiled for the first time since she'd come in.

'I thought you were going to charge me.'

In her presence he phoned a landlady from the town and booked her in.

'You'll like her – she's a very calm and comforting sort of person.'

The doctor's wife arrived with a pair of jeans, underwear and a maroon T-shirt which had been a handout at a conference on blood pressure.

'There's holes worn in the elbows of this sweater. But if it got cold you could push up the sleeves. That seems to be the style nowadays. You're welcome to have a shower first.'

'Then come into the other room for a cup of tea,' said the doctor.

'Or something stronger,' said his wife. The doctor stood up.

'Is that everything?' He went to the book on his desk and ran his eye down the page. He touched his pockets as if it would remind him of something. 'And what of him? The perpetrator?'

'I threw boiling water at him but it missed,' she said. 'All it did was make him more angry. Gave him more excuses. He had a knife – all I kept saying was I do not consent to this.' And again she was crying. Again he handed her tissues.

'Where is he now?'

'He just went on. To the north.'

'Did you know him?'

'No.'

'You're lucky to be alive, by the sound of it. Did you speak to him?'

'A bit. He said he was on the boats.'

'Everybody here's been on the boats. Except red-haired women.' The doctor put up his hands defensively when she looked up at him. 'Apologies. It's one of the fishermen's superstitions.'

Even though it was after eleven the bedroom was filled with a milky light. Things could be made out – the mirror reflecting the not-completely-dark sky, the Victorian picture of cattle drinking, the wardrobe and fireplace. There were still slivers of light in the west. It had been the longest day recently but she couldn't remember how long ago. The window was open an inch or two at the bottom and the net curtains furled and unfurled in the draught. The whisky was not doing the trick as the doctor had promised it would. Despite having had no sleep the night before she found it difficult to get over. She kept seeing him. Him. The fucking thug. To wrench herself away from such images was difficult. And the young men of the town did not help – gunning their engines and squealing their tyres as they cornered into the Square. When they drove off, in the silence which followed, she could hear the sound of geese. They were somewhere in the sea loch and the racket they made was halfway between lamentation and laughter. She'd never heard anything like it. Images of him kept leaping into her head making her angry. Sick, as well. She kept swallowing hard, keeping things down. It was hard to get rid of. His eyes. That upper lip. His stupid boy's knife. The pain he caused her. Maybe the urge to throw up was the tablets – or the alcohol – she wasn't used to the taste of whisky. She remembered it from childhood – from her mother's remedy for toothache. Whisky painted onto the hurting tooth. The doctor had urged her to a second drink and she knew she shouldn't have taken it because he poured them large. But when she'd seen all the paintings on the walls – abstract landscapes by Barbara Rae, still lives by Elizabeth Blackadder and Anne Redpath – she felt at home, expected maybe to see some work by her own parents there. And all the pills he'd shoved into her. And that injection. What was it? When she closed her eyes the bed raced backwards and she had to snap them open again to stop the sensation.

No, she wouldn't tell her mother – not a word. It would be too distressing for her.

The way he undid his belt with a kind of smirk. And set his binoculars on a rock. She jumped out of bed and closed the sash window, pushed it down with both hands. Thud. The sound of the geese lessened, the curtain was still. She got back into bed again. She smelt of something she did not recognise. The T-shirt belonging to the doctor's youngest. It had been laundered but somehow when it was against the heat of her body it took on a smell of its own. A foreign smell – a maroon smell – a smell whose source was now at the other side of the world. It wasn't offensive, just someone else. A woman. Having been raped and finding herself wearing another woman's clothes she felt somehow representative. One size fits all. She endured the condition of women across the world. That buckle sound of the belt opening and her incredulous oh no, he's not after that. There is no shame about being raped. If somebody punches you in the mouth or glasses you in a pub you're not *ashamed*. You're injured. It's not *about* shame. As he was taking off his jeans she made a run for it but he easily caught up with her on the flat rocks by her swimming pool and dragged her to the ground.

Gut knots again at the very thought. The cigarette smoke from his breath, from his clothes – and afterwards the chlorine stink of his seed.

'We can do it again. The other way round.' And he did, just as soon as he was ready. She lay as still as she could in the hope that he would not hurt her beyond repair and kept repeating that she did not consent, she did not consent, she did not consent to any of this until he punched her violently on the back of the head and her forehead struck the rock so hard she nearly went unconscious.

'Just fuckin shut up.'

Then she just cried with the pain.

She must try and think positively. Practically might be easier. Later in the summer she could contact the skipper and get him to pick up all her gear and her work – the drawings and the paintings, the Polaroids and the notebooks. She should be able to salvage something out of this disaster. She had no fears for the cat. She'd seen it kill and eat – voles or mice, she didn't dare inspect them too closely. What she hated was the way it played with its catch – letting it almost escape so many times before killing it. At night it was

183

breathtakingly fast catching and eating moths drawn by the light – once she was appalled to hear fluttering inside the cat's mouth before it chewed and swallowed. 'Oh cat how could you?' She'd never got round to giving it a name. When she'd left, it had been curled up by the fire, asleep. But would it get ticks in its fur – be weakened and eventually die? Or when she'd go back with the skipper would she meet this feral panther patrolling the place. Seeking whom it may devour.

The guy's face kept stabbing into her – the way he moved his upper lip as if he didn't believe a word she said. After the second time he got dressed and moved off by himself. He kept an eye on her from a distance. She cried herself out, then got dressed. What was she going to do? The stones which had pinned her washing to the rock were the right size but they were a long way off and there was nothing of a similar size here. And he was so strong and so fit. He would overcome her immediately. After a while he got to his feet and came closer, squatting in front of her.

'I bet you enjoyed that?' he said. She didn't say anything. He talked a bit. What amazed her was that he seemed to make so little of it. She hadn't consented – *at the beginning,* he seemed to say. What was all the fuss about? Why was she so bloody upset? Did she know how that made *him* feel? It was all natural – people fucked all the time. Day in, day out. Implied that it should make them feel closer. She would consent the next time. That's the way it happened in the movies. How long would that be? How long had she got? He'd done the sneering lip movement when she asked if she could take a photograph of him. One side of his lip went up. A bit like Elvis.

'Fuck off,' he said. He smoked a cigarette as he stared at her. 'You must think I'm a stupid cunt.' Then the lip movement. 'But it doesn't work that way. All I have to say is you were dying for it. Out here on your own, for fucking ages. With nothing but your thumb. And then daaa-dahh! I arrive. You become a raving knob jockey. Fuckin Miss Posh panting for it. So yeah – take my photie. Readers' boyfriends. You're so fulla shit it's coming out your mouth. And by the way, your art's bum cheese – I could do stuff like that – fuckin dire, man. I hope you can take better photos.'

The souped-up cars roared back into the town and parked by the square, their stereos pounding. Bub-bub-bub. Wailing rock guitars. Heavy metal screeching. Getting deep into her. Almost hearing with her stomach. Then they drove off again bub bub-bub and she heard the tyres yelp distantly as they cornered and zigzagged their way out of town.

The pillow was soft at her face. Sleep was close. Then all possibility of it disappeared.

'You fuckin stay where you are,' he said and walked back for the Polaroid.

'Don't think I'm going anywhere,' she said. Why did he think she could go anywhere? Her legs were like jelly and she could hardly move with the pain he'd left in her. But it might work. It would have to work. She was utterly convinced this guy was going to kill her when he finished with her.

He set the camera down in front of her. She got to her feet trying not to show her pain as she moved. She was sure she was bleeding at the back. He stripped off his T-shirt to show his lean and muscled upper body and stood with his back to the sea and sky, his knuckled fists on his hips.

'I like the body graffiti,' she said.

'What?'

'The tattoo.'

He turned his forearm to the camera and tensed it.

'I can do a close-up of that, if you want,' she said. 'Sit down.'

'Fuck – who's giving the orders round here?'

'Me,' she said. 'Put your top back on.' He put the white T-shirt on and sat down, leaning back preening himself. She went close to him, looking at him through the viewfinder. Would the blood show? But she kept her face simple. He lay back on his elbows with his knees wide open. She was shaking. She clicked the shutter and waited. The camera zizzed out a white print and she tucked it under her armpit.

'Lemme see?'

'Wait. The heat makes it quicker.' She counted. After about a minute she dropped it onto the rock in front of him. Head and shoulders with the blue sea behind him. He looked down at it but made no comment.

'Now one standing,' she said. He got to his feet and she moved in on him, close. 'To the left a step.' He did as he was told. She was giving him confidence in her. Hypnotising him. Holding up her hand for him to look at. She was trying out stuff she had seen other photographers do in the College. At one point she was doing so well she behaved as if she liked him. 'Eyes to the camera.' There was something terribly vain about him. Raising one eyebrow. She pressed the shutter and the camera expelled another print. She set it down on the rock to develop. Everything seemed to take ages.

'Why no armpit this time?'

'We've got all day.'

'You never spoke a truer word.'

When the print was ready he looked down at it.

'All right, man.'

'Now both of us,' she said. She set the camera on a waist-high rock and framed up the shot on him. 'Back a bit. Leave room for me. Watch the red light.' She clicked on the self-timer and began counting as she moved to where he stood. 'Ten, nine, eight.' His eye was on the camera watching the red light winking, arranging his face. The last couple of steps she ran. 'Six, five . . .' and she pushed him full in the chest with both hands. He grabbed onto her instinctively but she carried them forward with her momentum and they were falling. Toppling together. Both of them plunging deep into the water. She opened her eyes in the green depths to see where he was but saw only her own wake of white bubbles. Something touched her foot and she kicked out as hard as she could, scissoring her legs. The moment she surfaced she struck out to sea, swimming her fastest crawl. Then she turned and looked back. He must have kicked at the same time as the swell surged because his head and shoulders appeared and she thought for one horrible minute the sea was going to deliver him up onto the rocks again or that he had lied to her when he said that no one up here could swim and in fact he was actually a good swimmer – a strong swimmer. But the moving sea closed over his frantic head and he disappeared.

Next she was filled with a fear that he could swim to her underwater. And grab at her ankles. She waited treading water. The pain was still in her but now there was something else. The minutes passed. She continued to tread water – frog's legs. She waited and waited. He was nowhere to be seen.

'Yes,' she said to herself. She set out to swim to the beach.

On shore the first thing she did was to retrieve the Polaroid and the two pictures. There was a third picture hanging from the camera. It was of empty rock and sea. An absence. Two absences. Then she saw the binoculars. She flung them as far as she could into the sea. She left dark footprints and splashes as she moved over the rocks. She went back to the tent shivering. At this time of the evening the midges were beginning to annoy her. Her cheek-bones and the soft parts of her ears itched. To chase them she made the biggest fire she'd ever made and sat staring into it. She kept glancing behind her. If this was a Hollywood movie he would come back. Somehow he would be behind her the next time she looked around. Or the hand on the shoulder. Against all the odds he would have survived and would now be looking to punish her. Cut her throat. Sparks flew up into the sky and the burning wood cracked and spat.

Now, to do anything seemed the most enormous task. It took ages for her to unbutton her clinging shirt and take it off. She hung it on a stick. Steam began to rise from it almost immediately. She towelled herself dry and sat hunched and shawled by the fire, utterly weary. She felt she could not move. Even slightly. She daren't change any more. She daren't look to see if she was losing blood. She had ceased to exist from the waist down – except for the pain. Feed the fire. It'd get all the wood used up. She'd leave the next day. At some stage she summoned up enough energy to flick the two photos of him into the fire. They curled and burned with a pure blue fame. The picture of rock and sea and sky she kept. Towards morning she became cold and put on the dried shirt, and then was driven to get her mauve jumper and sleeping bag from the tent. The clothes she had on her were now dry partly from the fire, partly from her body. She remembered it as a night without sleep, yet she must have dozed with her head on her knees. Her memory of wakefulness and sleep became mixed with what was happening to her at present. Sleep was very far away, yet very close. Move a leg, rest her cheek on her forearm, turn on her left side. Towards the window, away from the window. A bed of soft nails. She might make the Polaroid the centrepiece of her exhibition – a picture with some rock and some sea and some sky. You never knew when sleep was close. Sleep was gradual. But it must be close because she hadn't shut her eyes for forty-eight hours. The human body needed sleep the way it needed food. Some shut-eye. It just could not be put off. Nobody died from sleeplessness. Lying there in your coffin with your eyes wide open. Able to die but not to sleep. Sleep and death were cousins. Shakespeare was always going on about it. Three layers – some rock and some sea and some sky. And nobody but her knowing the significance. Like that statement of the theme of a fugue. Variations to follow. Sky and sea and rock. Blue – grey – black. Solid – liquid – gas. And all stations in between. Light – half-light – dark. The doctor in his armchair after a few drams had apologised for being male – and his wife reprimanded him, saying it had nothing to do with gender and everything to do with misguided arrogance and brutality. Then they tried to pinpoint who the guy was. His age – on the boats – the knife. The doctor said his wife was also a doctor in the practice and knew more about the local people than he did. The boy she was thinking of hadn't far to go to seek his problems. She was almost sure she knew who it was. But then again, maybe not. How charitable. But the girl did not want to hear a name – it would have been too frightening to know a name. She wanted to get out of that sitting room before anything more was said. Before they became any more friendly. Moments came and went when she did not know whether she was asleep or not. Then she remembered the guy had seemed unable to smile – seemed not to know what it was to be amused – the muscles of his face were incapable of it. What a terrible thing to have happened. It had nothing to do with the remoteness of the place – that guy would have

hurt a woman eventually – maybe even killed her, whether
it was in a town or a city or a village like this. The doctor
circling her, stooping and looking over his half gold-rimmed
spectacles at her sex . . . a feeling not unlike blancmange or
tapioca . . . a solution . . . an urgency . . . she was late for
something . . . but the doctor's wife touched her hand, held
it for her and said there, there love . . . however momentary
. . . dreaming of insomnia . . . and blue sky and grey sea and
black rocks . . . and blue sea and grey rocks and . . .

The doctor, with his wife in the passenger seat, was driving
to the town at lunch-time. On the hill they met the funeral of
the drowned boy walking behind the hearse to the graveyard.
The doctor stopped his car and got out and stood to
attention. His wife did the same by the passenger door. He
recognised a few members of the family. Others were friends
and neighbours. People in such a small place came out to
show their respect. The father was pale – he was not crying
but you could see he had been crying. Unsteady. He was being
gripped under the arm and helped along by his brother. The
father looked much older than he remembered him. The doctor
had attended the house when the dead boy's mother was
terminally ill with breast cancer. After she died the father had
rolled up his sleeves and taken to the drink with some
determination. Looking at him now some twenty years later
it was remarkable how he had survived. But it was taking its
toll – it was in his face. The doctor had warned him many
years ago when he came to his surgery with an infected cut

on his hand. And he had spoken to him on the day he had
called to see his boy, sick with the measles and in danger of
developing complications. In the middle of the day the curtains
had been drawn in both the bedroom and living room – and
the father was lying on the sofa in front of the television barely
able to suck his thumb. With a sick only child in the house.
At school the boy was not liked – other children feared him.
Even the teachers were wary of him. A law unto himself –
going to school when he liked – skiving when he had better
things to do. Always getting into fights, and winning most of
them. The doctor had inserted more than a few stitches for
which the boy, and later the youth, was responsible.

Then there was a period of hope – after school when he
talked about wanting to join the Army. People said it would
straighten him out, give him a trade. But he was brought
before the Sheriff Court for causing a row on a bus and the
Army career fell through before it even started. It came as no
surprise that such a boy should die young and in this tragic
fashion. And then he remembered the girl who had come to
him one Sunday evening in early summer to say she'd been
raped. The doctor gave a little salute to the tail end of the
cortège and climbed back into his car. His wife did likewise.

'Sad,' she said. 'The father looks poorly.'

'Yes.' He turned the key and started the engine. 'Did you
do some forensic?'

'At Dundee – yes.'

'Hmmm.'

'Why?'

'How long do you reckon the boy was in the water?'

'Your guess is as good as mine. A month – maybe more. They say they relied on his tattoo for identification. He drifted thirty miles up the coast.'

'Yeah . . . but.'

'It depends on how cold the water is. Sometimes they don't resurface at all. But if you want to know when I think he drowned . . .' The doctor's wife trailed off. There was silence in the car.

The doctor said, 'The girl came to us in late June . . .'

'So what are you saying?'

'Nothing,' said the doctor. 'Not a thing.'

'I'm not saying anything either.'

He put the car into gear and his wife lightly covered his hand on the gear-stick with her own for a moment. She ended the gesture with a little pat. He moved forward down the hill. Through the windscreen they saw seabirds swing this way and that over the harbour. The masts of tied-up vessels criss-crossed and fenced as they wallowed and rocked in the choppy water of the harbour. In the rear-view mirror the funeral continued upwards to the graveyard.

* * *

Day 8.

Hot, idyllic weather. Blue sky and calm water. Tiny wavelets wash in – a kind of tongue roll – just one at a time. The sea is mirror flat reflecting the sky. Black and yellow bladderwrack breaks the surface between the dark rocks which are covered with tiny white pin limpets.

She leaned forward, slightly crouched. The handwriting on the tear-off pages was partially obscured by her brush strokes. But she read the words as if they were new, as if the diary entry was today's. She expected to feel the lightning flash of fear again, the surge of adrenalin, but it did not come. Neither did the hand on the shoulder.

On the far wall were two of the series *Self-portrait in maroon T-shirt*. In one the face recognisable but smudged – in the other a further disintegration which she now thought too much like a Francis Bacon. Out of the corner of her eye she noticed something bright flit across the wall and ceiling of the gallery. She looked at what it was, full on. A bright disc shimmering. She moved her wrist and the disc of light traversed the painting. It was the reflection from her wristwatch. She dismissed it – saw it as a good sign that she could remain calm. It was like the fairground attraction where you have to move a metal loop along a twisted wire from start to finish. If at any point the loop and wire touch there's a harsh electric buzz. Sometimes it was as if she was advancing the loop along her own jagged nerves waiting for the touch, the rasp of remembering. But now she was OK. She was capable of smiling.

The door of the gallery opened and the bell pinged. Voices. She was in the room with the Inverannich paintings and felt somehow guilty to be caught by strangers looking at her own work. The voices were American. An elderly couple. They approached the boy on the desk and wanted to know if they had to pay. He said no but invited them to sign the guest book. Were they on holiday? They answered, loudly now. They were not American but Canadian. From Halifax, Nova Scotia. Said that both their families were originally Scottish – how could they be otherwise with such names. 'My wife's a McKenzie. And I'm Campbell. Contrary to what people say,' the old man's voice had amusement in it, 'it was the brave who stayed.' They all laughed.

She stepped back and looked out at the desk. There was nothing remarkable about the tanned leathery faces and expensive spectacles. Both wore different tartan scarves. Souvenirs, no doubt.

They made their way into the rooms and began to look at the paintings. After each one the man stepped closer to read the painting's title aloud. As his wife gazed at the work she made disconcerting little noises with her mouth. The couple drifted into the room with the Inverannich works and the man blew out his cheeks. She hated being there, not declaring herself as the painter of these images. It was like overhearing herself being talked about. She had to get out. But they were friendly, wanted to declare their origins to anyone who would listen, wanted to acknowledge her, maybe share something with her in that polite North American way. The old man leaned towards her as she tried to sidle past him and said, 'Such images. Such viral images he's managed to capture.'

She looked at him.

'He?' The word was out of her before she could do anything about it.

'A woman painted these?'

'Yes – me.' She could have bitten off her tongue. He looked confused for a moment. Looked at his wife then back to the woman in front of him.

'They're your work? You're the painter?' She nodded but did not trust herself to confirm it by speech.

'That's wonderful.' He smiled.

'Yes, indeed,' said his wife. 'Wonderful work. You are to be congratulated.'

'Thank you.'

She began to make her escape, self-conscious that her block heels were making too much noise on the wooden floor.

MATTERS OF LIFE & DEATH 2

Visiting Takabuti

Nora woke. Her mouth was dry. The glass of water had grown bubbles overnight. She washed down her tablets and afterwards listened hard but could hear no rain, nor signs of rain. Rain would spoil everything. She swung herself out of bed slowly. These days she was like eggs. Too sudden a movement and she felt something would give. She'd been feeling like this for months now – but hadn't had the courage to go to the doctor. What could she say? Last time, after checking her blood pressure, he told her she was showing signs of osteoporosis – effectively her inner scaffolding was dissolving.

She eased herself into her slippers. They waited left on the left, right on the right just as she had withdrawn from them the night before. Outside it was dry. December dull but dry. She sat on the side of the bed thinking about the day ahead. It would be good to have the boys. She knelt and said her Morning Offering.

On the way back from eight o'clock mass she took in the milk from the door. She made porridge, not forgetting the salt, and watched it boil – plopping into holes, blowing gouts of steam. When it was ready she tumbled it into her

197

dish. Half a teaspoon of demerara sugar and the cream from the neck of the bottle. Porridge stuck to you – it set you up for the day.

Nora lived in a small flat above a dry cleaners overlooking the main road. She no longer heard the constant traffic. Occasionally she got the smell of the dry-cleaning chemicals but that was not unpleasant – a bit like petrol – but lately she had wondered if breathing this stuff, day in day out, could be good for her.

She put on her fedora-type hat, her good coat and knotted a cream silk scarf at her neck. Some strands of her white hair were sticking out and she tucked them in. On her lapel was a Celtic brooch of gunmetal and amethyst. She gave herself the once-over in the full-length mirror. She would do.

It was not far to her niece's place. She took her time, looking around her, nodding to various ones she knew.

'How do you do?'

'I'm grand. And yourself – how are you keeping?'

'Well – thank you.'

When she arrived she opened the door and walked up the hallway.

'Molly, it's only me.'

'Aunt Nora.' Her niece was at the kitchen table having a cup of tea and a cigarette.

'Where are they?'

'Out somewhere. I told them not to be long. And not to be getting dirty. Would you like a cuppa tea?'

'That would be lovely.' Molly made a fresh pot of tea.

'This is very good of you – taking them off my hands.'

'Don't mention it. Sure am'n't I the Aunt of Treats?' Every so often she would see something in the paper which would be suitable and would ask Molly if it was all right to take the boys. They'd gone to the pictures – to films she had previously viewed and approved. *Goodbye Mr Chips* and *Oliver Twist*. Tony – the older boy – said he'd had nightmares about Bill Sykes and his horrible dog, that white snub-nosed thing. The one time it went wrong was when she brought them to Joyce Grenfell on stage. This actress was supposed to be very amusing but she was unsuitable for young ones. Thank God the boys were innocent and they came out none the wiser.

'I wouldn't do it if I didn't enjoy it.'

'There's a lot they can learn over there.'

'You never said a truer word. It'll teach them a thing or two.'

Molly poured the tea.

'I mind the day you brought me. I didn't sleep for weeks.'

'Isn't it only natural.'

'Natural can be upsetting. I wouldn't let them see their Daddy.'

Nora raised the cup to her lips and sipped. She nodded as if she understood.

'And how are you?'

'On the up and up.'

'I'm glad to hear it. Are you all set for Christmas?'

'The Widows' Pension doesn't run to big presents.'

'If you're short I've . . .'

'I'll be just fine.'

A door slammed and there was a blundering noise in the hallway.

'Here they are now,' said Molly. Aunt Nora drank off her tea just as the two boys burst into the room.

'Hellooo – you two. Are you all ready for your wee jaunt?' They grinned and whispered to each other. Tony was twelve and his brother Ben was two years younger.

'Can we get sweets?'

'Who do you think I am – Carnegie?' Aunt Nora stood. 'So we're off to visit Takabuti.'

'Who?' said Tony.

'Who's he?' said the wee one.

'Get your coats on.'

How she loved them – the both of them. And their wee uprightness. With their grey socks and jumpers to match. Their mother scolded and wrestled them into their raincoats.

When their belts were tightened Aunt Nora held each of them at arm's length.

'Window models – would you look at them. Mr Burton would be jealous.'

As they stood at the bus-stop she talked to people she didn't even know – about the weather. The boys looked down.

'You're easy embarrassed.' And they smiled and continued to turn away. 'Don't they look well? Fine and dandy.'

'Is that their names?' People at the bus-stop laughed. The seventy-seven came, the only bus to go across town.

'Upstairs?' said Tony. Aunt Nora pulled a face and nodded. The two boys dashed up ahead of her. She held onto the metal rails with both hands and hoisted herself up each steep step, complaining. The boys were together in a seat halfway up the left-hand side. Before she sat down the bell rang and the bus started. The back seat was empty and she half fell, was half catapulted into it. When she got her breath back she called out to the boys to ask if they were all right. They nodded and went on talking to each other.

It had been years since she had travelled upstairs on a bus. You could see so much more. Across the trees to the ponds in the Waterworks, the green hills beyond.

'Boys – look at the swans,' she pointed and they turned. 'The man swan is a cob and the lady is . . . ?' The boys didn't know. 'A pen. A female swan is called a pen.'

She wanted to add something about swans devoting themselves to the same partner throughout life but thought it unsuitable for boys of that age. And of no interest. She had retired from teaching some twenty years ago – or was it thirty? If she'd married she would have had to resign her post. That was accepted in those days. But she never did marry.

Her own schooldays had ended at fifteen when she was asked to stay on as a monitress. Then she'd gone to the newly opened St Mary's Training College on the Falls Road. Her first school had been on the north coast – in Ballintoy. It had been such an excitement – to be on her own in digs. With the McBrides. Nicer people you couldn't meet. She'd admired their youngest son, Arthur, almost from the beginning. His manliness, the light in his eye, the comical way he said things. 'There's no use hurrying if you don't know the times of the trains.' He had the north-east accent which made his sayings even funnier. 'A man's a man for all what?' he would say and laugh.

He was about the same age as herself and was working in a pharmacist's shop in Ballycastle. She smiled. *The Encyclopaedia of Primary Teaching*. She'd talked so much about it he'd offered to buy it for her. But she wanted to be independent. She saved everything she could from her early wages and sent away to England for it. The best money she'd ever spent. It came in three bound volumes containing methods and lesson plans and 'pedagogical advice'. In a separate black box – illustrations relating to the lesson plans. The pictures had a great variety – some were famous paintings, *The Death of Ophelia* and *And When Did You Last See Your Father?*, some were drawings – Dürer's *Hands in Prayer*, others were diagrams – the best way to light a camp-fire, a cross-section of a burial chamber in an Egyptian pyramid. In Ballintoy she had an easel at the front of the class on which she set such pictures. The children had walked to school in the rain, their clothes were grey, their slates were grey, as were the walls. The colours of the illustrations on the easel were vibrant, like stained glass.

The first time she had permitted Arthur McBride to kiss her was on the deserted and windswept beach at Ballycastle.

The sand was racing, as was her heart, at the things he was saying. And they stepped into the lee of Pans rocks and he kissed her as she held her hat to her head. Such was his caution – she had been staying with them for almost a year – because he feared his action was too premature. If she did not feel the same way it would spoil his chances of walking out with her again. He later said he feared the loss of her company, more than anything. And she could not understand this – what else was there, apart from her company?

She had come this same journey two weeks ago to check that everything would be all right in the art gallery part of the museum. She had turned into one room and there in front of her was the most brazen picture she had ever seen. She had taken out her glasses and examined the label. *Somebody-or-other at her toilette.* The painter was French, of course. This bare-chested woman towered above her. Hester or Esther. She was stretching up to knot her hair, exposing even her armpits. The painting must have been six foot tall and it was done in the most realistic detail. She stared up in a kind of irritated amazement at it. A uniformed guard was pacing slowly around the room. He drew level with her.

'Is this on permanent exhibition?'

'Yes it is, ma'am.'

'Thank you.'

She would have to find another route.

*

By now others had come onto the top deck of the bus. A man in the seat in front of her read his newspaper. There was a photo of the Prime Minister on the front page. How could he take the country into war again so soon? Over such a thing as the Suez Canal. It had only been ten years. There should be no more wars – ever again. Because men will die and there will be widows and grieving sweethearts.

The bus was approaching Shaftsbury Square.

'How am I going to face those stairs?' Aunt Nora shouted to the boys. People turned. The boys' faces went red. She ordered them to ring the bell and go down the stairs in front of her 'to cushion her fall'. They were to take their time and on no account were they to let the bus move off until she was on the pavement.

She got down from the platform by herself and put her hands on the boys' shoulders.

'Holy mackerel. What a handling,' she said. The bus drove off into the traffic. She gathered them close, one on each side, to cross the busy junction.

The boys walked on in front, sometimes running and mock fighting, other times quietly in step.

'Would anybody like an ice cream?' The two turned. 'Cones or sliders?' They opted for cones. 'Watch you don't dribble on your coats – or your mother'll crucify me.'

They passed the University – red-brick gables set back behind green lawns. She felt the effect of such expansive and well-kept lawns was to hold the public at bay. How dare you – the grass said. The boys finished their ice creams and walked on the waist-high perimeter wall, their arms out for balance. It was tricky enough not to trip because there were still the stumps of metal railings which had been sawn off during the last war and never replaced.

'Careful,' she called out.

After the Great War she moved back to Belfast and taught in St Anthony's in Millfield, a poor part of the town. The windows of her classroom were of frosted glass except for the topmost pane and when the children had been set a task she would sit and stare through this pane at the battleship grey of the corrugated-iron roof of the parochial hall. Sometimes she cried – if she felt it coming on she turned her back on the class and pretended to look at the book shelf. She had developed the knack of weeping in silence. When it passed she removed her handkerchief from her sleeve, blew her nose and regained her composure. Only then did she turn to face the class.

The boys were setting a good pace on the wall and she began to feel a little breathless. She had worn too many clothes and was beginning to perspire a little. She liked 'there' journeys because they seemed shorter. 'There and back' journeys were a different thing. The farther you got from home the farther you had to go back.

In the middle of the driveway, in front of the University's main door was a memorial for the Great War – a winged female figure holding up a wreath which she is about to put on the head of a young soldier. Arthur McBride. All those years ago. He had enlisted without telling her. At the time it was the thing to do because the country was in a good mood and proud of itself. The place was flag mad – especially in Belfast. When he said goodbye to her, he took both her hands in his and kissed them. Adieu, he said to her left hand. Adieu to her right. Then her lips. Adieu. She often wondered why he had chosen the French. He was of a poetic turn of mind – very fond of Burns and had many of his songs off by heart. But to say goodbye that way? She told him that she loved him and only him. She promised never to love another.

In the Museum she made the boys hang their coats in the cloakroom. They'd feel the good of them when they went back out. She hung up her own coat but kept her hat and scarf on. In the middle of the entrance hall was a massive marble statue of a seated Galileo. The boys stood whispering in front of it. A statue of Robert Burns 1759–1796 was in the corner. 'Ae Fond Kiss' came into her head. 'And then we sever'. How cruel and clever of Burns to rhyme it with 'for ever'. Because Arthur never came back. His family got word that he was missing in action. And they told her because they knew what was between them.

'Aunt Nora,' Tony was trying to get her attention. 'Where first?'

'This way,' she said.

The roller-ball clock was beautiful, glittering as it moved. The boys put their faces close to the glass case. It was an inclined metal plane with a shallow groove, along which a silver ball rolled, zigzagging from one end to the other. When the ball reached the bottom it struck a catch reversing the tilt and rolled back the way it had come. Each journey took a known amount of time and the hands moved on accordingly. She got her glasses out. When she snapped the case shut it popped too loudly and echoed. She read out the label for them. 'These clocks were not novelties but were serious attempts at timekeeping before the introduction of the pendulum.' The air was full of small mechanical sounds, tickings and scrapings.

She led them from room to room – pointing out what she thought would interest them. A one-hundred-and-thirty-five-million-year-old amethyst geode from Brazil – like a shark's mouth jagged with jewels instead of teeth. A ball made of rock crystal quartz 'for looking into the future' she said in a mysterious voice. Fossil sea scorpions that were four hundred and twenty million years of age – imprinted in shale.

'And you're only ten,' she said to Ben, winking.

'Ten and a bit,' he said. 'Nearly eleven.' His voice was pitched high.

'So you are,' she smiled. 'So you are.'

The boys crouched to stare into the glass eyes of stuffed animals.

'How lifelike,' said Aunt Nora. Brown hares standing on their hind legs boxing. White hares in their winter coats, hiding in the snow. The boys straightened up and wandered the corridor ahead of her.

'Left here,' she called out. There was a sign for a café. 'Would you like a lemonade?'

She sat opposite them drinking her tea. They had bottles of lemonade with straws – two in each bottle for greater purchase – and were sucking hard, indenting their cheeks.

'Easy,' she said. 'No noises when you reach the bottom.' The boys looked at each other and tried not to laugh.

'No bottom noises,' said the wee one. Then they did laugh.

'It comes down your nose – the fizz,' said Tony.

'Oh don't . . . please.' There was silence except for the noise of spoons being dropped one after another into a drawer in the kitchen. 'Are you looking after your mother these days?' They both nodded. 'Good – because she needs a great deal of looking after. She's only a slip of a girl herself.' She blew a thin stream of air to cool her tea and sipped it.

Tony said to her, 'I liked the clock with the silver marble.'

'The hares were brilliant. Boxing.' Ben bunched his wee fists and faced his brother.

'There's more,' said Aunt Nora.

'What?'

'Wait and see.'

When they were finished they set off again along polished corridors. She felt refreshed having taken the weight off her feet for a bit.

'Don't go running ahead,' she said. They walked beside

her until they came to a doorway. She ushered them into a room where the blinds had been partially drawn. It was still light enough to see photographs on the walls – of the Sphinx with his lopped-off nose, the pyramids, boats sailing on the Nile. There was nobody else in the room. A glass case stood in the middle of the floor and Nora called the boys over.

'Meet Takabuti,' she said. The boys tried to see. 'She's been dead for two and a half thousand years.' There was some kind of black creature in the case. Wrapped in biscuit-coloured bandages.

'It's a mummy,' Tony whispered to his brother. Both of them stared wide-eyed. The thing was completely wrapped except for its head and a withered hand. It wore a cape of blue earthenware beads. The hand, thin as a backscratcher, had stained the wrapping it rested on. Her lips were liquorice black but slightly open showing white teeth. The nose, a snapped-off beak.

'What's it made of?' the younger boy asked.

'It's a real dead person.'

'What?'

'Dust thou art and unto dust thou shalt return,' said Aunt Nora.

Lying beside the mummy was the decorated lid of her coffin. The idealised face – painted with gold and black and scarlet. Beside it – the dead thing.

'I don't like it.' The smaller brother pulled a face and walked away to look at something else. Tony followed him.

Nora was left standing by herself looking down into the

case. She was so small. Shrunken almost. But she could have been a beauty once – with such white teeth, skin of alabaster. Walking in sandals by the Nile. She said a prayer for Takabuti, that she might be in heaven no matter what her faith.

She leaned her forearms on the glass and felt a great weariness come over her. The life she had lived now seemed barren and worthless. Everything she had taught would soon be forgotten. She had brought no children into the world. Maiden aunt to two boys was the most she could say. Today she had brought them to visit Takabuti and the lesson hadn't worked as well as she had hoped. They were not as shocked as she had been when she first saw her. The children's voices were now distant. Something was happening to the sounds. They were the way sound was when you listened to a shell. Distant seas. There was a sour taste in her mouth. Her heart skipped a beat and had to race to catch up again. She reached out and leaned her fingertips on the glass case for balance. Little haloes of condensation formed around each finger as she braced herself. She held on – until the dwam gradually disappeared.

Tony's voice was very close now.

'Mammy said we should get home before the rush hour.'

She looked at her watch. It was coming up to four o'clock. The light had almost disappeared. It was either night or the rain coming on. Or both.

On the way home the boys went to the upper deck – by now she was only fit for downstairs.

'Behave yourselves,' she had shouted at the disappearing legs. The conductor was standing by the stairs. She said, 'Old age is not for the faint-hearted.' The rush hour hadn't started yet so there were plenty of seats. The conductor came to where she was settling.

'Are you going far?' he said.

'All the way,' she said and laughed. 'And the two boys upstairs.' She paid the fares and arranged herself. It was warm inside the bus. The darkness and the rain were on the outside. The throb of the engine and the shudder was comforting. Warmth was a pleasure – whether it was in bed or beside the fire or with her hot-water bottle. The traffic lights changed and reflected their colours on the wet pavement. She began to feel drowsy and moved closer to the window.

She tried to think about the mummy and the gilded case. The container and the contained. And it made her remember the Irish story – of the soul that kissed the body. At the moment of death. She had first heard it from Arthur McBride at a wake in Ballintoy. His eyes were bright trying not to be moved as he told it. The soul leaves the body and tiptoes to the doorway. Then turns and goes back to kiss the body that has sheltered it all these years. Day in, day out. In sickness and in health. In grief and in joy.

And Nora imagines it happening at her own death. She sees it like cinema. The soul, in her own image, leans over and with tenderness kisses her empty body. Adieu. And each time the soul makes the journey to the doorway reluctance takes hold and it returns to kiss the body with its shrunken frame and its frail bones of honeycomb. Adieu. Three times in all. From one vital part of herself to another. Adieu.

When it came to their stop the two boys ran down the stairs. They shouted to their Aunt Nora on the lower deck but she seemed not to hear. Tony went to her and she was still, her head in its hat pressed against the window, her skin a grey colour. The conductor came to see if he could help but there was nothing he could do.

WINTER STORM

He was wakened by the noise of the heated air rising from the vents in the bedroom floor. He got up and opened the curtains. The windows looked out into a wood of silver birch. Here and there were patches of snow which had not melted. Two squirrels were careering from one tree to another across the thinnest of branches. Up or across – it seemed to make no difference to their speed. From the other side of the house bamboo wind chimes created a faint but constant sound. Above the garage was a clock face with a single hand for temperature. It was twenty-two below.

It was amazing how folk had found ways to live in such inhospitable places. There was another bedroom where the owner had switched off the heating. For weeks now the windows had been opaque with patterned frost – on the inside. Each screw-nail in the wood frame had grown ice crystals as long as eyelashes.

On the wall above the bed was a modern painting by a Pawnee artist. There was Native American Indian stuff all over the place – wood carvings, a woven war shield and in the hallway a pair of snow shoes like bad tennis racquets pinned to the wall.

He checked that the telephone was firmly in its cradle. He picked it up and listened for the dialling tone then, on hearing it, replaced the receiver.

He was the only one at the bus terminus with grey hair. The others around him were Asian students. People his age and American students owned cars. When the bus arrived he got a seat by the window and flipped back his hood. The window seat mattered little because everything in the American Midwest looked the same. He found it hard to get a sense of history. The motor car dictated everything, swept everything aside. Businesses and shops had to have acres of parking space so that the town appeared spread out, flat, diluted – little more than a series of neoned fast-food places, telephone wires and car parks with the huge sky arched over everything. Buildings from the turn of the century were rare. People had told him of the prairies before the first colonisers came through. This was territory to be crossed as quickly as possible – the wet lands, the bogs, the seven-foot-high grasses. The air black with midges and flies. It was hard for him to imagine the place they described. Then one evening, as he stood waiting for his bus, he looked up high into the sky and saw countless thousands of crows, flapping slowly homewards out of the sunset. A huge flock with stragglers and outriders edging across the yellow sky. And he was aware that this was a thing that had happened every evening for thousands of years. He could have been – not a Scotsman at a bus-stop

– but a Kiowa-Apache on horseback looking up, moving south, anxious to be away from such a winter.

Before the stop on the north side of the campus the girl beside him put on her mittens, covered her mouth and nose with her scarf and pulled her hood up. He got off behind her, tugging his black woollen hat well down over his ears. At home in Scotland he would be laughed at for such headgear. But here in Iowa, Midwest people seemed to wear anything in winter – even Norwegian knitwear. Which meant that he had difficulty lusting. It was hard to tell the sex of students from the eye-slit they left in their clothing. Bright colours were no indication that the wearer was female.

His room was on the south side of the campus, as far away from the bus-stop as it was possible to be – far enough away for him to classify it as 'exercise'. He burrowed down into his coat for the long walk. The university buildings were around the perimeter of a central green space, large as a public park. At least it was called a green space even though the winter grass was dead and biscuit-coloured.

Paths criss-crossed the park forming a lattice-work from one building to another. Between classes the central acres became thronged. The students reminded him of skeins of geese – moving Indian-file. At the intersection of several paths he always thought it remarkable that, like birds, they didn't bump into one another. Every time he came to a junction he was wary, measured his step, slowing down or speeding up as need be, to avoid a collision with another person.

The halyard on the flagpole clacked loudly as he passed

and the Stars and Stripes stood out straight in the wind. It made a noise almost like rattling. The clock in the campanile chimed ten but he didn't look up because the icy wind was coming from that direction and it would sting his eyes. He kept his face turned away. At the halfway point he passed the emergency telephone.

As he entered his department building the first snow was beginning to blow in the wind. He cleared his throat. From past experience he knew his voice sounded peculiar when he didn't use it for a long time – it could shift a whole register or not come out at all. The last thing he'd said was 'Goodnight' to the girl in the office the previous evening.

'Good morning,' he said. The throat clearing had worked.

'And how's our Scottish poet today?'

'Professor to you.'

She smiled. It was she who had typed his name into a slot on his door – 'Professor Andrew Younger' – when he'd first arrived.

'Thanks for the promotion,' he'd said. His room was on the lee side and before he took off his coat he went to the telephone. He tapped in the voicemail code fully expecting to be told, as he had been told almost every morning of his stay, that he had no messages. 'You have one new message,' said the female recording. He had to sit down when he heard Lorna's voice as clear as anything from Scotland. She was sorry but she'd mislaid his home number – surely he hadn't changed houses again? The point was she'd been offered another subbing job at the same school – somebody else was pregnant. Whether or not it was because it was a Catholic school she hadn't a clue. But it was an offer she felt she had to seriously consider. The money was excellent. So it was a real possibility that she wouldn't be joining him in sunny Iowa. She had to say yea or nay by the end of the day. It could have been such an adventure. However she would see him when he came back in the summer. Maybe she would try and ring him later.

He sat in the chair for some time, then replaced the receiver. At the window the snowflakes rose and dithered. He took off his jacket and knitted headgear. He wore his hair in a pony-tail – had done since he could remember. There was a small oval mirror beside the door and he checked his appearance before going along the corridor to the kitchen beside the office. It was empty. He poured himself a coffee in a borrowed mug and dropped one of the larger coins into a basket – was it a quarter or a dime? This was the brush-off. How could she do this – after what they'd agreed? She was so obdurate. He'd said that to her one day, 'You are so fucking obdurate,' and wondered why she had laughed out loud in his face. Back in his room he sat down in front of his screen.

He switched on his computer and while it went through its warming-up noises he sat with his head in his hands. He had promised to write a CV for a campus radio show he was to be on. He gave a minimum amount of his history and listed the titles of his collections of poems – his 'slim volumes' as Lorna called them. 'Weight watchers' poetry.'

Now and Again
Holidays of Obligation
Making Strange
Like Everything Else

How futile all this was. How was anyone to deduce his life from such fragments? He'd been married to a girl called Cathy for three years in the sixties. She'd worked for the Abbey National but it had all broken up when she went off with her branch manager, himself married. The only good thing was that there'd been no children. After that he'd had a succession of occasional relationships – until he'd met Lorna. She was widowed with two grown-up sons who were away at university – in Hull. Then in her early forties she herself decided to go to university. That was where he'd met her, one night in the bar after he'd done a reading. Andrew wanted to settle down with her but she was wary of commitment and wanted to keep her own place. And her own pace. So he visited a lot. And slept over. After a couple of years they began to become routine and still she wouldn't commit. She seemed to say, 'This is fine as it is – but don't push it.' When he was offered the poet-in-residence at Iowa State he hesitated but Lorna said he MUST take it. It was too good an opportunity to miss. Besides it was only for a year. Not even a year – September to May. Lorna had said it with such conviction that he wondered if she wanted rid of him – that this was the moment she'd been waiting for.

She was now a Modern Studies teacher but did mostly

subbing because of the freedom it gave her. Her present contract
was due to have run out sometime after Christmas and she
had promised to give serious thought to following him to Iowa.
Then they had this terrible falling out. Fights are never about
what causes the fight. They are always about something else
– something in the past, an irritation, a vengeance, a reprisal.
He'd gone round to her place to watch *A Doll's House* on
television. They'd settled with a glass of wine, she curled up
on the sofa beside him. Then the cat had *wanted* out. That
had to be made absolutely clear. And the other fact – that the
outer storm doors were bolted shut because of the kind of
night it was – is also relevant. If the storm doors were not
closed against an east wind then the porch inevitably flooded.
That wonderful actress Juliet Stevenson was in the lead role
of Nora. It didn't seem like a long play but it was – and the
only thing that distracted Lorna's attention was the rain against
the windows. And the wind. She kept remarking it. Then the
play ended with the boom of Nora closing the door as she
left. Lorna went to look for the cat and, not finding her
anywhere in the house, opened the front doors and it came
streaking in, thin as a greyhound because of the wet.

'Did you know the cat was out?'

'Yeah, I let her out earlier.'

'Why didn't you let her in again?'

'We were watching the play.'

'She's been out for hours. In the rain.'

She got a towel and began to rub the cat down in front
of the fire.

'You're shivering, pet.'

'Cats don't shiver.'

'Tell him. You're shivering, aren't you, darlin.' The cat's fur looked jagged. 'He's a bastard of a poet. Cares about nobody but himself. Here, love. Easy.'

'I hate the way you utterly sentimentalise animals.'

'Then you can fuck off. Back to your own place.'

He thought of Juliet Stevenson when he slammed the door on his way out. Before he left for America he'd tried to patch things up. But only with limited success. She seemed cold – couldn't care less whether they got back together again or not. As for him, he couldn't wheedle because . . . well, because it was wheedling. There were certain things couldn't be said out loud – 'I want someone to talk to, to share things with. I want sex and companionship. I want you, Lorna, to be with me. To complete me. You have all the things I lack.'

There was a knock at his door.

'Come in.'

It was the cleaner. Twice a week she excused herself and emptied his waste-basket. She was a Native American Indian woman, very big with a solemn leathery face. She had a trolley loaded neatly with brushes and shovels, sprays and polishes. She didn't smile when he greeted her but adjusted the muscles of her face to show him that she was returning his greeting. She reminded him of the tall Indian in the movie of *One Flew Over the Cuckoo's Nest*. The one who

never spoke. She took his waste-basket to her trolley and
upended it. Nothing much came out.

He said, 'It's *so* cold today.'

She set the basket back on the floor.

'You betcha,' she said and went out. Her metal shovels
clanged like low-pitched wind chimes as she moved down
the corridor.

He finished the CV and began to type up his notebook
from the weekend. He'd written quite a lot. When he ate out
he'd choose from the menu then jot things down until his
food arrived. It was a way of having a conversation with
himself. Writing in the notebook was a way of not being alone:

*Shop at the Hy-Vee just as it's getting dark. The clear
sky is amazing, almost like a tinted windscreen – pinkish
rising to green then to navy. The evening star is low and
as bright as a plane headlight coming at you straight on.
Met a girl student today called Ellen Lonesome.*

*Walking down Hickory Drive I look up and see that in
this country Cassiopeia has become an M rather than a
W. And somebody has upended the Plough onto its handle.*

Here people don't cook food, they fix it.

*Remembered a phrase of rejection of my mother's today
at lunch. 'The back of my hand to you.' If I failed to
keep a promise to her or let somebody down and she
was really disappointed she'd say it.*

The snow fizzed as the wind whipped it at the window
pane. He looked up but could only see the leaden grey sky.

'Will it lie?' In Scotland it was the first question asked when the snow came on. Here it always did.

At lunch-time he went along to the kitchen for another coffee. The last woman in the office was putting on her coat. All the others had gone.

'Didn't you hear the weather warning?'

'No.'

'Oh really?' she said. 'Campus Radio have been at it since morning. They don't expect it to quit until after midnight.'

He went back to his room and stood looking down through the window at the snowstorm. The paths were covered now. He sipped his coffee and sat down in front of the computer again. He checked the phone in its cradle. He should write to Lorna – put it on paper. Elegantly. To see if she could be tempted by words. But then it would be too late. This afternoon decisions would have been taken. He could ring her but she would be in class. And if there was one thing she hated, it was to be phoned at school. Trekking along corridors behind that stork of a school secretary.

He stood up to look out. Maybe he should go. He couldn't see to the ground and the trees outside his window were no longer visible. Yes, he should go. And not wait for a phone call. She'd only said 'maybe'. And if she was getting rid of him she wouldn't want to talk to him directly. He saved what work he'd done and snapped the Off switch on the computer. He put on his coat and zipped it up to his throat.

The only one in the corridor was the Native American

cleaner mopping to and fro. Pulling an apologetic face he tiptoed over the wet floor.

'I'm off,' he said.

'You betcha.'

Somewhere there was the sound of a distant flush and a woman from Linguistics came out of the ladies' restroom.

'Hi – I thought everyone had gone,' she said.

'Not me.'

They walked together as far as the lift and she pressed the button.

'The University is officially closed this afternoon,' she said.

'Why's that?'

'That's why,' she looked towards the window at the end of the corridor. 'It's a rare event – to close down.'

Both of them turned from the window and stared up at the indicator lights.

'I think this elevator's bust,' she said. They went down the stairs. At ground level he turned off as she continued to the garage in the basement.

'You don't have a car?' she said.

'No.'

'Oh really?'

'The bus does me fine.'

'Are they still running?'

'I hope so.'

'Which side of town are you?'

'West – out by the river.'

'Oh – I'm the other side.' She hesitated. 'Can I offer you a ride?'

'No – no thanks. Not with the roads the way they are.' She nodded and jackknifed her hood up into place.

'Take care,' she said.

He waited until he was at the front doors before putting on his stupid hat and gloves. His boots squidged on the terrazzo. Even with the doors closed, papers swirled in the draughts of the hallway.

The snow had silted up the steps outside, evened them to a slope. He wound his scarf around his mouth and nose, Bedouin style, and went down the steps. He breathed in and, at about the third breath, felt the hairs in his nose begin to stiffen and freeze. It was an odd sensation, a bit like having too much Coca-Cola. He turned left and headed along the path. In some places the snow was forming into drifts, other places there was no snow at all. The path in front of him was swept clean by the wind. It was so *bitterly* cold. He had never felt anything like it. At home in Scotland there was a damp cold that got into your bones and joints but this was different. This was thermometer cold. The wind ripped at the skin of his cheeks. He partially closed his eyes to protect them and kept his head down. Now the path disappeared into the snow. He couldn't tell where the edges were. So he just kept walking straight. Each time he put weight on his boot the snow creaked beneath his sole. He looked round to check on the direction of his footprints and noticed that he could no longer see the building he had just come from. It was a white vortex.

'Fuck me,' he said. His prints were fast disappearing as the wind evened them out. The snow was so fine it got everywhere – particles the size of salt. His wrists were feeling numbed. The wind got at the skin space between his gloves and his sleeves. He tried to put his hands in his pockets but it didn't help. With his eyes narrowed he now found difficulty in seeing. His eyes had begun to stick. His tears were gumming up his lashes as they began to freeze.

'Jesus . . .' He jerked his eyes open, widened them quickly so that the icing was broken. He'd had 'mucky eyes' as a boy and in the morning he'd have to open them with his fingers. It was like that now, hard to see into the wind with the ice on his lashes. There was also a terrible roaring of the wind around his head, cuffing him this way and that, probing his hood and the thin knitted hat. His boot sunk down to his knee in a rise of snow. His other foot followed and the drift covered his knee. It was getting deeper. This can't be right. It has only been snowing a couple of hours. He didn't want to look at his watch, to bare his wrist. He tried to calculate how long – four hours at the most. The snow was even, uninterrupted when he looked round for any sign of the path.

He heard a noise in front of him – a kind of stuttering – and for a moment he couldn't think of what it was. A rattling. Then he saw it was the flagpole. With its halyard vibrating in the wind. But the flagpole shouldn't be there. It was in the middle of the fucking green. How could it have moved to the path? He stopped and reached out and touched the metallic pole with his glove. He looked up but could only see glimpses through the driving snow of the flag at the top of it.

He knew the path was to the right of the flagpole so he headed back to join it. The wind had loosened the scarf protecting his face and it blew out in front of him. He tried to cover his face again and stuff in the end of the scarf at his neck. But his gloves were too big and insensitive for him to do it properly. He stumbled into a drift of snow and lost his footing. But he didn't fall far – this snow was up to his thighs and it was soft. He keeled over, more than fell. 'I'm too old for this kind of a caper,' he said out loud. 'What the fuck's going on here?' He clambered upright. Because of the fall, snow had got inside both his gloves and up his sleeves. As it melted his wrists felt wet as well as cold.

Now the skin of his cheeks felt numb. He tried to protect himself from the wind by cupping his hands like horse blinkers at each side of his face. But this exposed his wrists again to pain. He looked back at his tracks and headed into the unbroken snow. Then he heard the gonging of the campanile. That must be the hour. Two o'clock. He had been out here the best part of fifteen minutes. Normally, at a good pace, it took him about eight minutes to cross from one side to the other. The sound was coming from his left, which was as it should be. Or *was* it coming from his left? The wind kept plucking and distorting it – was it an echo he was hearing? It was like trying to tune in an old radio.

Then he heard another sound – distantly. The long slow hoot of a train. It appeared to be coming from his left also. But this could not be because he knew the tracks ran along the west side of the campus. He decided to keep going straight ahead. The sound could not be trusted.

The sheeting snow eased momentarily and he saw a clump of trees in front of him. Ah! He stepped into the shelter of one of the trees. Here the snow was over his boot mouth. Which particular group of trees was this? He tried to remember – there were groups of trees all over the place. Scots pines with the longest cones he had ever seen, evergreens with swishing fronds which he thought would do for whisking at flies if he stayed till the hot and humid summer, ornamental trees with burnished bark the colour of copper. But this was a group of trees he couldn't remember seeing – these were like silver birch. There was a bench of polished stone or marble in the middle of the copse which was still miraculously free of snow. Along the back of its seat the words:

AFTER TILLAGE COMES THE OTHER ARTS

Then in smaller gold lettering:

DONATED BY THE CLASS OF 1932

He sat down on it with his back to the wind – and thanked the class of thirty-two.

Fucksake, this was getting serious. He was completely disorientated and his cheeks were beginning to hurt or to go numb, whichever was the more dangerous. He was panting for breath and the tears in his eyes were freezing and icing his bottom lids to the top ones. He was too old for this kind of nonsense. He debated whether or not he should turn around and go back to the department. Maybe stay there till the thing had blown over. But the woman in the office had said the forecast was for it to continue snowing until midnight. There was a sleeping bag on the top of the book shelf in the room they'd given him. So it had happened before. He could stay the night. It was a piece of fucking nonsense that he couldn't get from one side of the quad to the other. He felt so tired. Tired out of all proportion. Maybe lie down on this marble bench. He took off his gloves to get a handkerchief to dry his face. He put his hand in his right pocket but he was astonished to find it full of snow. And it was frozen. He had not buttoned the pocket flap down properly. Somewhere beneath the snow he located the handkerchief, took it out and tried to wipe his face. But the hanky too was stiff and frozen and felt like sandpaper or broken glass on his skin. He put it away again. His left pocket was in the same state. He'd better get on, now that he'd got his breath back. Get the bus. Get home and make a cup of coffee. Turn up the heating. Maybe have a hot shower. Step out on the tiles with the underfloor heating. There was an enormous gust of wind which blew his gloves off the bench onto the ground. He grabbed at one but saw the other cartwheel away into the snow. Hand over fist. It was the right one he'd saved. The left one had disappeared completely.

'Jesus . . .' He cleared his left pocket of snow and put his hand into it for protection. The inside lining crackled and felt like cold tinfoil. He could maybe find the glove tomorrow. Or in the spring.

He hunched his shoulders and stood up. All he had to do was continue walking in the same direction – to walk in a straight line – across the diameter of the park – and he would get to buildings of some sort at its circumference. The snow in this place was so deep he was having to lift his knees to make each stride. Could this really be the path? Off the beaten track, for fucksake. It was laughable. Except that he hadn't enough breath to laugh. He was panting with the effort that was required of him now to keep going. He wanted to stop, to lie down. To curl up and sleep. The most bizarre things were coming into his head. He laughed. Where was the emergency telephone? What fucking use was an emergency phone if you couldn't find it? He had not thought much about it, assuming, because it was equidistant from all buildings, that it would be for violent situations at night – an assault or rape or something. It had a red push button and a built-in mouthpiece for speaking into. Yelling into, maybe. If he could find that he would definitely use it. He wouldn't feel shamefaced about using it – because now he felt he was in some difficulties. No, I'm not being raped – I'm just lost. Yes, somewhere in the middle of the fucking campus. Then he remembered someone telling him about the habit of Midwestern farmers in weather like this, who tied a rope from the house to the byre for fear they'd get lost going to feed the beasts. And another story about a father and son who tied themselves together in case they'd become separated in just such a storm.

He *must* be at the other side by now. The snow on the ground here was blowing, forming into ribs like sand at the seashore. Something loomed up in front of him and disappeared just as quickly. He moved towards it. It was another flagpole. He leaned up against it. But he could only remember one – in the centre of the quad. There wasn't another one. Maybe he'd forgotten the second one. He looked up. This one was flying the same flag as the one earlier.

'Fuck it.' It *was* the same one. He must have walked in a circle.

He remembered a childhood game in which adult hands had grabbed and blindfolded him. Then they turned him round and round until he didn't know where he was. He'd stand, his arms outstretched, his fingers moving, listening to the breathing of the grown-ups. When they took the blindfold off he was always astonished at where he was in the room. And once memorably when he opened his eyes they had tricked him into a different room altogether.

He hunkered down to make himself less of a target for the wind and snow. He would have to try to extricate himself. But there was no guarantee that he wouldn't do exactly the same thing. In another fifteen minutes he could be blundering past this fucking flagpole for a third time.

He must conserve his energy. His feet were now totally

numb and his left wrist was causing him pain. The scarf around his mouth had become saturated with his breath and refrozen so that it was white and brittle against his lips. Where any outer material came in contact with his skin, it was abrasive. His cheeks felt like raw meat and he wondered if they were bleeding.

If the flag was at the centre of the quad . . . He looked down but the prints he had made on his previous visit were completely obliterated. The wind direction was of no help because it was swirling and twisting . . . But neither could he take no action. Staying there was not an option.

If he found the emergency phone he would ask to be connected to long distance. Was it still called that? Lorna, get me outa here. I'm fucking lost. We can patch it up. We can make a go of it. I want somebody to share my life with. Somebody to come home to. His mother's phrase was now in Linda's mouth. 'The back of my hand to you.'

He got slowly to his feet. His gloved hand almost stuck to the metal of the flagpole. He arbitrarily chose a direction and set off. He was blundering now. Flutters of panic mixed with a couldn't-care-less attitude. Why was he so fucking tired? Monumentally tired?

He tripped on something and fell flat on the snow. He looked back to see what it was in the kind of stupid way you do. It was the path. The wind had cleared the snow and the concrete edge of the path was sitting proud of the snow. Ho-ho-ho – he now had a fifty-per-cent chance of getting to his destination. Follow the path. That way he would either end up at the department or reach the other side. Then he remembered that this is what he had done the first time. The path would disappear under the snow. He lay there wondering if he should get up. His face was against the snow. The carillon sounded. It must be a quarter past. Or was it half past? How long had he been blundering around out here? Surely to Christ a grown man could walk across a quadrangle – even if it was as big as a park. He looked to his left and saw a pair of boots. Then upwards to a padded coat. A hooded figure bent down and took him beneath his armpits, helped him to his feet.

'I must have slipped,' he said.

'You betcha.'

He tried to see the eyes behind the slit in the hood. He guessed it was a woman from the voice. She was tall and bulky or else she was wearing a lot of clothes. It was the Indian woman, the cleaner from his department.

At first she took his arm but, when she felt him walking steadily, she let it go. She looked closely into his hood.

'You from Scotland?'

'Yes.'

'You gotta phone call. Nobody else in the bildin.' She shouted above the howling of the wind, 'She said to tell you. She's coming.'

He sheltered in her wake as she walked the blizzard in a straight line to the buildings on the far side.